HIS MISTLETOE
PROPOSAL

HIS MISTLETOE PROPOSAL

BY

CHRISTY McKELLEN

MILLS & BOON

First published in Great Britain 2017
by Mills & Boon, an imprint of HarperCollins*Publishers*
1 London Bridge Street, London, SE1 9GF

Large Print edition 2018

© 2017 Christy McKellen

ISBN: 978-0-263-07352-2

MIX
Paper from
responsible sources
FSC **FSC™ C007454**
www.fsc.org

This book is produced from independently certified
FSC™ paper to ensure responsible forest management.
For more information visit www.harpercollins.co.uk/green.

Printed and bound in Great Britain
by CPI Group (UK) Ltd, Croydon, CR0 4YY

Okay, Charlotte, my compassionate, clever, beautiful girl. As promised, this one is dedicated to you.
I love you more than words can say.
And I always will.
Mum

CHAPTER ONE

To my darling Flora—confidante, cheer-leader and anchor to my universe,

So this is weird, right? Me speaking to you from the grave. But I wanted to get all my thoughts down on paper because I knew I'd get all choked up and make a mess of it if I tried to say it out loud. So here goes...

I know this is a lot to ask, but please don't be too sad now that I've gone. I feel as though I've made peace with what's happened to me and I'd hate to think of my passing as some-thing that would hold you back from living your own life to the full. I've had a good and happy existence. All twenty-eight of my years have been blessed with love and wonderful experiences and my life's been all the better for having you in it, Flora.

I'm so proud of you for all that you've achieved. I always knew you'd be successful in whatever you did, but your drive and determination have astounded even me. I know you probably won't take a minute to step back and see the enormity of what you've accomplished, but get this: you truly are an incredible person, as well as the kindest, most generous woman I've ever had the pleasure of knowing.

Which leads me on to two favours I have to ask of you, Flora. Firstly, and I know it's a biggie, please look out for Alex now that I'm not around to do it any more. As you know, I was the only family he had left and I hate to think of him being alone in the world. He wouldn't admit it—I think he was trying to protect my last few weeks on earth so they'd be stress-free—but I think someone broke his heart recently and he's really hurting.

Secondly, check your breasts for lumps EVERY DAY. Or, even better, get a gorgeous sex-god to do it for you *wink*. Don't make *the same mistake I did and shrug cancer off as something that happens to someone else. Someone older. Or less busy.*

You have such a good heart, Flora. You deserve to be happy, so go easy on yourself, okay?

I love you.
Your best friend for ever,
Amy

FLORA MORGAN CAUGHT the tear on her finger before it fell onto the precious, now rather crumpled, piece of paper she clutched in her hand. She'd carried the letter around with her ever since it had dropped through her letter box nearly a month ago, and she'd taken it out regularly since then to read it, hoping to conjure Amy's spirit during her weaker moments.

She missed her friend so much it made her heart physically ache. She had no idea how she was going to live her life without having Amy around, always ready to jolly her out of a funk and lift her spirits with one of her rousing pep talks.

But she was going to have to. Because her best friend was gone.

The hum and chatter of Bath's famous Pump Room restaurant faded away as she lost herself in some of the happy memories she'd shared with Amy during the six years they'd known each other. They'd met at their first jobs after graduating from university, sitting side by side in cramped, scruffy cubicles at the blue-chip company based in Glasgow that had selected them for their highly competitive fast-track programme. They'd hit it off immediately—their mutual love of order and precision drawing them together like paper clips to a magnet. Sharing both the professional and personal exciting highs and painful lows over the years that followed had cemented their tight friendship.

Folding the letter carefully away into the Italian leather handbag she'd bought herself for a birthday present, Flora took a deep breath to centre herself. Now wasn't the time to get all emotionally tangled up. She needed to focus on her reason for being here today and for that she needed to have her wits about her.

Not that her reason for being here today had turned up yet.

Sitting up straighter, Flora became aware of a burst of movement over at the maître d's desk and she turned to see that her companion for afternoon tea had finally arrived. Eighteen minutes late. But then who was counting?

Shaking off her lingering melancholy, she straightened the neckline of her silk blouse and smoothed her fingertips over her eyebrows to make sure they were both still following the required curve. They were.

Standing up, she tried not to notice how out of place Alex Trevelyan seemed in jeans that looked about ready to lie down and die, black Chelsea boots with scuffed toes and a crumpled leather jacket. She doubted very much that he'd even glanced in the mirror that morning considering how his mussed-up chestnut-brown hair fell over his cobalt-blue eyes and what must have been a week's worth of stubble darkened his prominent cheekbones and square jaw.

A few years ago, his just-rolled-out-of-bed sexy musician charisma would have been irresistible to her naïve, overly optimistic self, but not any more. She'd learnt her lesson about men like that the hard way. If she dated anyone these days, she went for smart, business-orientated men who were just as focused on their careers as she was. Though, as Amy had regularly pointed out, that was probably why she'd remained mostly single for the last couple of years. Which Flora was fine with. She didn't need a man to fulfil her.

As he drew nearer, Alex's bloodshot eyes ringed with dark circles made her heart squeeze. She mentally berated herself for being so critical of his appearance when the poor man's twin sister had died barely a month ago. He was obviously still grief-stricken.

She'd only seen him briefly at the funeral; he'd turned up at the last second wearing casual grey trousers and a bright blue shirt that had been open at the neck and glaringly free of a tie. To be fair, Amy hadn't wanted them to wear the usual black mourning clothes. Afterwards, he'd been busy with the vicar and a group of people whom she'd guessed were old friends of the family. She, in turn, had been caught up talking to mutual acquaintances of her and Amy's. By the time she'd looked round to offer her condolences to Alex he'd disappeared, not even turning up at the wake afterwards. She'd guessed he'd been too upset to face any more sympathy from strangers.

Amy's words swam across her vision—*I was the only family he had left*. He needed her support and kindness right now, not her judgement.

Relaxing her posture so that her hands fell neatly to her sides, Flora gave Alex her warmest smile as he finally navigated past the last couple of linen-covered tables and came to a halt in front of her. Taking a deep breath, she was just about to launch into the short monologue she'd composed in her head about how pleased she was that he'd agreed to meet her so they could talk about Amy and support each other during such a difficult time, when he leaned past her to pick up her glass of mineral water and proceeded to chug the whole lot of it, not even acknowledging her presence until he'd satisfied his thirst.

'That's better,' he gasped, slamming the glass back down onto the table before finally turning to face her with a wink. 'Don't let anyone talk you into drinking whisky after four pints at the pub. It's a life event catalyst.'

She stared at him, aghast.

Instead of looking contrite, he yawned loudly into his hand. 'Sorry, I've only just got up. Late night.'

Flora swallowed back her shock before replying, 'It's three o'clock in the afternoon.'

He smiled, his expression one of wry audacity. 'Like I said, late night.'

This wasn't the grieving, broken man she'd been expecting to turn up today and the incongruity was playing havoc with her composure—something that made her really uncomfortable. She hated to be on the back foot; years of facing difficult clients in tense business situations had taught her that.

Pulling herself together, she said, 'Thanks for meeting me. I thought it might be nice for us to get to know each other, what with us being the two people closest to Amy.'

He nodded, then motioned for her to sit down, taking the seat opposite.

'You were in the States, right? New York?' he asked once he was settled.

'Yes, I was working as Head of Marketing for Bounce soft drinks,' she said proudly. 'I transferred over there when the company opened up a New York office about a year ago.'

Usually when she mentioned her job and the position she held, people would look impressed and start asking her questions about what that entailed and how she'd risen so quickly up the ranks, but Alex didn't say a word. And he didn't seem impressed either; he seemed…bored.

This didn't surprise her though; Amy had told her all about her brother's attitude towards people who worked for corporations and how he thought it was 'capitalist gluttony with a corporate greed cherry on top'. Flora privately thought that a man who had given up a perfectly good job in corporate finance to faff about as a musician had no right to judge others and their career choices. If he wanted to waste his talents just so he could sit on his high horse, looking down on others who were slogging away to make a success of themselves, then that was his business.

She wasn't going to rise to it. She had more important things to worry about—like gaining the trust and respect of her new boss. After transferring to the London-based office it was proving harder than she'd expected to do this.

Not for the first time, it had made her question whether she should set up her own business at some point, but she was keenly aware of what a big risk that would be.

She gave herself a mental shake. She really shouldn't be allowing her thoughts to wander back to work right now.

'Anyway, since I'm over here now I thought it might be nice for us to get to know each other a bit so we could support each other,' she said, waving for the waiter, who appeared not to notice her. Biting back a sigh of frustration, she refocused on Alex, who was lounging back in his chair with his arms folded and his brow furrowed.

Was it her imagination or did he really not want to be here?

She cleared her throat. 'I didn't want to be one of those people who kept away for fear of not knowing what to say to someone who's just lost someone close to them,' she said, deciding just to plough on. 'Sending flowers and cards is all very well, but sometimes you just need some human contact, you know?'

He cocked his head and gave her a slow grin. 'Is that why you came back to England? For some human contact?'

She shifted in her seat, feeling heat rise up her neck. 'I needed a change of scene,' she said, straightening the cutlery on the table.

What she didn't tell him was that *he* was the real reason for moving back here. She was determined to take Amy's last wish seriously, and if that meant living in the same city as Alex for a while then so be it. London was too far removed from Bath to keep an eye on him easily, and she certainly couldn't have done it from New York. So she'd jumped at an opportunity for a temporary transfer to the West London office, commuting in from Bath to oversee a UK-only product launch.

Alex appeared to be thinking about what she'd said, and after a short pause he leaned forwards in his chair to look her right in the eye, as if making the decision to finally engage with the conversation. 'It's good to meet you in the flesh,' he said, the corner of his mouth lifting into a grin. 'Amy talked about you a lot over the years.' He paused. 'And during the last weeks of her life.'

At last there was a flash of emotion in his eyes, which he blinked away quickly.

Flora nodded, taking a moment to relax her throat, which had tightened with sorrow at the sound of her best friend's name. 'It's good to meet you too. I—' She took a breath. 'I feel awful that I didn't make it back in time to see her in the hospice. I tried to get back to England as fast as

I could, but—' She'd run out of words. The pathetic ring to her excuse made her cringe inside.

She'd thought she had more time. That Amy had more time. Her friend had told her during one of their regular video calls that she was doing better and not to worry about rushing back to see her. But then she'd taken a sudden, unexpected turn for the worse.

As if he'd read her mind, Alex leaned forwards and put his large, warm hand over hers where it lay on the table.' 'Don't beat yourself up about it. None of us realised she'd go that soon. She did seem to have a reprieve at one point. You couldn't have known. Amy knew you would have come sooner if you'd been able to. She told me that.'

Flora could do nothing but nod like one of those tacky toy dogs you saw in the back of cars sometimes. She was suddenly terrified she might start crying in the middle of the restaurant and have to sit there with her make-up running down her face and nowhere to hide.

Alex obviously read her distress because he gave her hand a squeeze. 'Hey, let's get out of here. This place is making my headache worse.' He glanced around the magnificent room with a pained grimace. 'There's a really good pub round the corner that does amazing burgers.'

Wrestling her emotions back under control, Flora shot him a bewildered look. 'But we've come here for afternoon tea.' She gestured round at the magnificent eighteenth-century room with its cut-glass chandelier hanging from the ornate ceiling and the grand piano, which was being expertly played by a gentleman in a tuxedo.

He wrinkled his nose. 'For a tiny plate of overpriced cucumber sandwiches? Sorry, but that's not going to cut it for me today.'

'Actually, this place is known for having one of the best—' But he'd already stood up and was waving for the waiter to bring the bill.

Deciding not to fight him on this—she wanted to keep things as friendly and light-hearted as possible considering why they were meeting each other today—she gritted her teeth and stood up, taking her purse out of her bag ready to pay for her drink.

He spotted her pulling out a twenty-pound note and waved it away.

'I'll get this.'

'You don't have—' But he'd already taken the bill from the waiter. He proceeded to rummage in his pockets to produce a handful of coins, which he emptied into his hand.

'Thanks, man,' he said. 'Keep the change.'

The waiter gave him a tight smile, then walked away, no doubt cursing them both for being the most awkward customers of the day.

Outside the Pump Room crowds of shoppers were stopping and starting along the pavement, as every now and again someone would halt at one of the little German-style wooden huts belonging to the large Christmas market that had taken over the whole of the city centre.

'Wow, it's busy out here,' Flora said as they waited for a break in the flow so they could join the slow-moving crowd.

'Warm inside the throng though,' Alex said with a smile. 'Free heat.'

He was right. Despite the biting cold of the day,

it felt cosy and comforting being encased in the large mob of people. There was an excited, almost magical, feeling in the air too, no doubt an eagerness for the upcoming festivities.

Flora had spent many years in her youth loving the excitement of the run-up to Christmas, but she felt nothing but numbness about it now. It was all too tangled up with the fallout from her last serious relationship.

Pushing away the wave of gut-churning despondency she always felt whenever she thought about that, she looked round and focused on a stall selling silk scarves in every colour of the rainbow, taking comfort in the beauty of the sight.

'So you live in Bath but work in London?' Alex asked as they walked away from the scarf stall, stopping at the next one along to peruse a tantalising display of mince pies and Christmas cakes. Alongside them an assortment of delicious-looking pastries covered in snow-white icing gleamed in the soft winter sunshine.

She nodded. 'Yes. I commute into Paddington

and the office is only a ten-minute walk from there. I felt like taking a break from living in the middle of a big city,' she said, telling herself she wasn't exactly lying by saying that. Recently she'd started to think that living outside the city where she worked would be better for her health. She'd be less inclined to pop into work at the weekends and less likely to stay as late in the evenings if she had to catch a train home.

Looking round at Alex, she realised that he wasn't even listening to her, but smiling at the pretty young stallholder instead. 'Nice buns,' he said to the woman, giving her a wink and making her blush and giggle coquettishly.

Flora rolled her eyes at the stallholder's reaction to Alex's cheesy pickup line. Okay, he was a good-looking man, she supposed—he had the same smile as Amy, which could light up a room—but the guy was a rumpled mess.

He turned and caught her staring at him.

'What?' he asked.

'Nothing. It's just—'

'Yes?'

'You don't seem—'

He appeared frustrated with her lack of words. 'What? Sad, bereft, miserable? Just because I'm not bawling my eyes out in public doesn't mean I don't miss my sister.'

Prickly heat washed over her. 'I know that. I wasn't criticising the way you're mourning her.'

'Weren't you?' He gave her a look that made guilt pool in her stomach. 'I promised her I wouldn't let grief get in the way of getting on with my life and I intend to keep that promise. She'd hate it if *either of us* was sitting around moping.'

'Yes, okay.' She held up her hands as a peace offering. 'I understand that. I guess it's just taking me longer to adjust to life without her, that's all.'

His expression softened and he flashed her his beguiling smile, making something twist oddly in her stomach. 'Fair enough. I know how close you two were. I don't mean to criticise you either. Each to their own, I suppose. I've chosen to move on with my life. It doesn't mean that I don't think about her all the damn time.'

Flora gave him a sympathetic smile, her guilt dissipating a little.

'Come on, let's get to the pub,' he said, gesturing to somewhere off in the distance. 'I could really do with a hair of the dog.'

Nodding, she fell into step alongside him on strangely wobbly legs and they rejoined the crowd, moving slowly onwards.

Alex Trevelyan took a deep breath and willed his heartbeat to slow down as he and Flora pushed their way through the dense throng of Christmas shoppers.

He really didn't want to be here right now. His head was pounding and he was having trouble keeping a smile on his face after Flora's insinuation that he wasn't mourning his sister properly.

From what he'd seen of her so far, he was surprised this rather uptight woman could have been such a good friend of his sister's, until he remembered the look of near reverence on Amy's face when she'd described Flora to him.

'She's really something,' Amy had said with enthusiasm. 'She comes across as a bit—' She'd paused, searching for the right word, her nose wrinkling with the effort. 'A bit spiky, I guess you'd say—especially if you don't know her well. All the people where we worked were intimidated by her.' She'd smiled as if remembering her friend's tyranny fondly. 'But underneath she's got a heart of gold. You'd like her. Honestly.'

It was the 'honestly' that had spoken to him. Knowing his sister as he did, Alex knew that it meant she wanted him to like Flora, but wasn't sure that he would.

Well, he could see now why Amy might have been sceptical. He wasn't entirely sure that he *did* like Flora, with her side-eyeing and staid pragmatism. Though he'd be a liar to say he didn't find her physically compelling. Who wouldn't, with her long sweep of shiny caramel-blonde hair and big grey-green eyes. She was definitely an attractive woman—though more because she made the most of her assets rather than being a stop-you-in-your-tracks beauty and she had a magnetism that kept drawing his gaze back to her. She was dressed as if she was going to a business meeting rather than getting a bite to eat with a friendly acquaintance though. And she was just so polished. Everything about her shone, from the tips of her manicured nails to the toes of her high-heeled leather boots. Wealth and good taste seemed to exude from every pore of her being.

She was not his usual type at all. He preferred women who weren't afraid to get their hair wet in the rain or get covered in mud on a long walk through the woods. He liked natural and down-to-earth and simple. Like his ex-girlfriend, Tia. The woman he'd thought he'd spend the rest of his life with.

Pushing away the sinking feeling that thinking about his ex created, he stared blankly ahead of him. He'd moved on now. There was no point in looking back. He'd promised Amy he wouldn't do that.

As they walked on, he noticed Flora turning her

head from side to side, as if trying to take in as many of the Christmassy sights as possible. The magic of the season held no allure for him at all this year. In fact, it would be fair to say that he was looking forward to the month of December being over and done with. Christmas Day was only going to remind him of how alone he was now.

'Take a left here,' he said into Flora's ear, attempting to cut through the noise of the crowd as they approached the side street leading towards the pub. The expensive scent of her perfume wafted into his nose, making him shiver in the strangest of ways. It had been months since he'd been in intimate contact with a woman and his body seemed to have gone a little haywire from the absence of it.

She nodded in acknowledgement and they moved slowly towards an opening in the crowd.

He watched her sashay ahead of him—elegant but entirely self-aware.

It made him think about something else Amy had said about Flora. 'I worry she's losing herself in her ridiculous quest for perfection.' Well, that fitted with what little he'd seen of her so far.

He wondered what else he was going to discover about her before the end of the day.

CHAPTER TWO

FLORA TRIED NOT to wrinkle her nose at the smell of stale beer that seemed to rise up in waves from the ugly red-and-brown patterned carpet as they entered the gloomy pub that Alex had insisted on bringing them to.

'I'm going to order a burger at the bar. Want one?' Alex asked as she settled herself at one of the sticky mahogany-stained tables, trying to avoid sitting on a suspicious-looking brown stain on the vinyl padded bench.

'Er…no, thanks. I'll just have a drink for now.'

He gave her a bemused frown, then shrugged. 'Okay. What would you like to drink then?'

She thought about it for a moment, then decided that alcohol might actually make this situation a little bit easier. 'I'll have a pint of the local cider.'

His brows shot up. 'Really? It's pretty potent stuff.'

She bristled. 'I might look like a lightweight, but I bet I can drink you under the table.'

'Now there's a challenge,' he said, grinning at her before turning away to head over to the bar.

She watched him charm the barmaid, wondering how on earth she was going to successfully insinuate herself into his life without it looking really suspicious. She was pretty sure he'd be entirely resistant to the idea of her keeping an eye on him if he knew that was what she was really here for.

He was so different to Amy, she mused while waiting for him to come back with the drinks. It was odd, considering that they'd both been brought up in exactly the same environment at the same time. But then she and her younger sister weren't exactly alike either. Violet was vivacious, artsy and beautiful, the total opposite of her: sensible, conventional and, if she was being totally honest with herself, only modestly attractive. Violet had always cast Flora into shadow whenever she was around; she was just one of those people with a natural *joie de vivre* that drew people to her.

Men, particularly.

An uncomfortable tightness had formed in Flora's throat and she coughed to clear it as Alex finally returned to the table with her cider and a pint of lager for himself.

'Thanks,' she said, forcing her mouth into a smile as she took her drink from him.

He gave her a nod and sat down in the chair opposite. 'Are you sure you don't want anything to eat?' he asked.

She shook her head. 'No, thanks. I'll have something when I get home.' She really didn't fancy eating here. Their table looked as though it hadn't been wiped in ages, which didn't give her much confidence in the state of the kitchen.

Picking up her drink, she took a few good gulps of it. The alcohol warmed her as it rushed down her throat to her stomach, lifting her spirits a little.

'So how long have you been living in Bath?'

she asked, watching him knock back half of his own pint in one go.

His eyes met hers and she saw a reaction in them that she couldn't quite decipher. Wariness, maybe?

'Just over a year. I was in London for a long time, but then I got together with the band I play with now. They're mostly based in Bath, so it made sense to move here so I could practise with them more easily.'

'Amy told me you play jazz.' She hadn't meant that to sound so derisive, but she'd never understood the lure of jazz and couldn't imagine how anyone would want to listen to it every day, let alone make a career out of playing it.

A flicker of annoyance crossed his face, but he didn't pick up on her disparaging tone. 'Yeah, we specialise in thirties-inspired jazz and blues, but sometimes we give our sets a more modern slant if we're in the mood and the occasion calls for it.'

'And how's it all going?' she asked, this time making sure to keep her tone upbeat. 'Is it fulfilling? How do you make it lucrative? Do you play at weddings and parties?'

He gave her a look that made her stomach clench with discomfort.

'It's not all about the money for me.' He rested his arms on the table. 'Look, I know jazz isn't to everyone's taste, but it's worth giving it a chance before you write it off,' he said bluntly.

She wondered whether there was an underlying meaning to that. *Don't write me off until you know me better*, perhaps. He had a point, she supposed. It was wrong of her to judge before she had all the facts.

'Perhaps I could come to one of your gigs some time?' she said, trying to pull back favour.

He nodded and smiled in a manner that made her think he was just humouring her. His food arrived then and he thanked the server, then tucked straight into it as if he'd not eaten in days.

This wasn't exactly going how she'd planned. She'd really not expected him to be like this: so... *blasé*. If she so much as thought about Amy, her whole body flooded with a heavy sort of dread and she had to think about work or something practical so as not to start welling up.

There was a good chance he was burying his pain though, so she needed to be patient and vigilant—ready to support him as and when he needed her.

'You okay?' Alex asked after finishing the last bite of his food, his satisfied expression morphing into a worried frown.

She realised with a start that she'd been staring at him.

'Fine. Just thinking about my week at work,' she lied.

'Want to tell me about it?' he asked, though she could tell from the edge in his voice that he was really hoping she wouldn't.

Pushing aside a sting of hurt, she shook her head. She didn't want him to know how difficult she was finding it to impress her new boss. 'I'd rather just forget about it,' she said, picking up her drink and taking a few more gulps of it for courage.

He nodded but didn't say anything.

'So when is your next gig?' she asked, trying to keep her tone light and conversational.

'In a couple of weeks,' he said, spinning his now-empty glass between his hands and glowering into the distance, as if picturing it unfavourably.

'You know, I really would love to come,' she said.

He turned to shoot her a look of deep scepticism. 'I got the impression it wasn't your type of music.'

She felt her face heat, embarrassed now by how dismissive her tone had been. 'Yes, well, perhaps I should give jazz a chance.' This struck her as funny for some reason. 'Hey, you should work up a marketing campaign with that as your strapline. *Give jazz a chance.*' She guffawed at her own joke, but for some reason Alex didn't seem to find it funny.

Grump.

'But seriously,' she said, rearranging her features back into a sober expression. 'I really would like to come and support you.'

'Well, that's very selfless of you, Flora, but I'm afraid the gig's sold out.'

'Oh.' This news shocked her. Perhaps he was more successful than she'd realised. She squinted at him suspiciously. Or was he just telling her that because he didn't want her there?

'Can't you get hold of extra tickets as one of the band members?' she asked. Surely he'd be able to swing something? She really wanted to show him some solidarity. She felt sure Amy would have approved of that.

'Nope. Sorry. I've already given all of mine away,' he said, standing up so suddenly it made her start. 'I'm going to the bar again—want another one?' he asked, nodding to her much-depleted drink.

'Well, I shouldn't—' she hedged. The alcohol had already had quite an effect on her, making everything look a little hazy and causing her to slur her words a little, but it was plain he was determined to have another and she didn't want to leave just yet '—but hey, it's Saturday, so why not?'

He gave her a curt nod and headed over to the bar without another word.

His denial of her request for a ticket to his gig still stung and she pondered how to get him to stop resisting her attempts at being friendly.

What would Amy have done?

She probably would have been upfront about the things he was trying to conceal and forced him to discuss them. But could she really talk to Alex like that without getting his back up? She didn't have Amy's light touch and easy wit— the woman could have talked the birds down from the trees—and she didn't want to blow her chance of getting closer to him.

It was obvious that he needed a friend right now though, judging by the way he wasn't taking care of his appearance.

She watched him slouch back over to where she sat, his body language self-assured but just a little bit weary.

He gave her a questioning look and she realised that she had been staring at him again.

'Are you sure you're okay?' he asked with one quizzical brow raised.

She gave herself a mental shake. 'Yes, fine. Are you?'

He blinked slowly. 'Yes. I'm fine, thanks, Flora.'

'I was just thinking you looked a bit worn out.'

He sat down, rubbing a hand over his eyes. 'Yeah, well, I've not been sleeping well recently.'

'Hmm, I'm not surprised. It's been a difficult few months for you, hasn't it?'

He shrugged, then took a sip from his drink. 'I guess.'

Apparently subtlety wasn't going to cut it. She considered hedging around the subject of his failed relationship, which Amy had alluded to in her letter, but decided she might as well just go for it and see what happened.

'So are you seeing anyone at the moment?' she asked, attempting an offhand tone.

His shoulders stiffened at the question. He folded his arms, then frowned, as if something had just occurred to him. 'Amy asked you to keep an eye on me, didn't she?'

'No!' The lie came out before she had time to modify it. 'I was just wondering, that's all. Being friendly and taking an interest.'

'Mmm-hmm.' He looked at her steadily for one long, loaded moment and she felt her cheeks start to heat.

'Okay, yes!' she burst out defensively, unable to handle his intense scrutiny any longer. 'Amy mentioned that you'd recently split up with someone and that she thought you were a bit cut up about it.'

'I see. So that's why you really called me, is it? To make sure I wasn't about to jump off the Pulteney Bridge?'

Flora shook her head jerkily. 'I wanted to see you so we could talk about Amy. You were the person that knew her best after all.' There was an uncomfortable beat of silence while she took a shaky breath. 'And I miss her.' She felt the tears start to well in her eyes again and blinked them back. No way was she going to cry in front of him now.

Her words seemed to have had some sort of effect on him, because his posture relaxed and he reached over the table to put his hand on her forearm. Her skin tingled alarmingly under his touch, but she didn't pull away. He probably needed some human contact too, she reminded herself.

'Okay, yes.' He sighed, a rueful smile appearing on his face.

'Yes what?' she asked, a little lost.

'I am fairly recently out of a relationship, but I'm fine. I was cut up for a while because I thought it could become serious, but it didn't work out. It's okay though. I'm fine. Still in one piece,' he said, taking his hand off her arm to thump his chest right over his heart.

His bravado had a false ring to it though. Maybe it was the repeated use of 'fine' or perhaps it was the flash of pain in his eyes that he hadn't quite managed to conceal.

Her resolve strengthened. Obviously he was still hurting but wasn't willing to talk about it with her. Well, she could bide her time. Perhaps once they'd got to know each other a bit better he'd soften and let her in. He probably needed to talk it all through with someone he trusted, and she was more than willing to become that person.

If only he'd let her.

Alex sat back in his chair with a sigh, feeling the burger and beer boosting his blood sugar levels and improving his irascible mood.

When Flora had questioned his relationship status he'd been ready to close her down fast, but had checked himself at the last minute. It was pretty clear she wasn't the sort of person to take a brush-off lightly—she had fire and determination in those big, bright eyes of hers. He'd decided that an approximation of the truth would be the best course of action.

Hopefully she'd leave it at that now. He didn't feel like rehashing the pain and misery of the last few months to satisfy the curiosity of a near stranger. Just because she'd been Amy's closest friend didn't mean she deserved his total trust and honesty.

Except it sort of did.

He sighed to himself, thinking back to the conversation he'd had with his sister in the hospice, the day she'd passed away.

'She may seem as tough as nails,' Amy had said, her voice weak and slurred from the pain-killers they'd been pumping into her, 'but she'll need a friend once I've gone. Promise me you'll be kind to her, Alex, especially if she comes to you looking for atonement. She'll beat herself up about not being here to say goodbye.'

And it seemed his sister had been right.

It also looked as though he was going to have to keep the hurried promise he'd made to her as he'd watched her life ebb away.

He remembered now how her request had seemed like the only positive thing at a time when he'd felt so horrifically impotent, unable to do anything to save his sister. It had given him just a little sliver of power over the situation. He suspected Amy might have known that too.

'I'm just going to the bathroom,' he said, suddenly feeling an overwhelming need to escape from the poignant memories that were pressing in on his head like a vice.

'Okay,' Flora said, producing an overly bright smile, as if sensing his pain.

In the gents bathroom he stared at himself in the mirror, noting the dark rings around his bloodshot eyes and the unhealthy pallor of his skin. He'd not meant to get so drunk last night, but he hadn't had the willpower to say no when his bandmates had suggested going to the pub after rehearsals. He'd also not been entirely straight with Flora earlier when he'd suggested that someone else had persuaded him to drink whisky until the early hours of the morning.

He'd done that entirely of his own volition.

Yesterday had been a difficult day and he'd felt the overwhelming need to get out of his head for a while and drown his raging thoughts. Music was usually his salvation, but it had become increasingly difficult to lose himself in it over the last few months and it was slowly driving him insane.

He slapped his cheeks, seeing colour bloom on his pale skin. Time to pull himself together.

Returning to the table, he bit back a wry smile

as he noted how uncomfortable Flora looked perched on the edge of the bench, as if afraid that sitting on it fully might sully her impeccable image.

'I swear that's the last time I drink whisky straight from the bottle,' he said flippantly as he sat back down, noticing Flora flinch a little. It reminded him of her less than impressed reaction earlier when he'd told her he'd only just got up. He'd laughed it off at the time but, truth be told, he'd found it virtually impossible to drag himself out of bed today.

They sat in awkward silence for a moment, both sipping from their nearly empty pints.

'It's no wonder you're depressed if you spend all your time in places like this,' Flora said suddenly in a voice that she'd perhaps meant to be jokey but actually came off as a little officious.

'I'm not depressed,' he stated firmly, feeling discomfort flood through him.

'Really? Are you sure? From what you've told me it sounds like you could be.'

He sighed in frustration, wishing she'd change

the subject. 'If I need a shrink, I promise you I'll give one a call.'

She ignored his pointed sarcasm and waved a hand at him, her movements suspiciously exaggerated. 'You know, it can be a great help to get out and socialise after ending a relationship.' She took an audible breath. 'Perhaps if you went on a couple of dates? It might give your spirits a bit of a lift.'

He stared at her in disbelief. 'Are you serious?'

Fixing him with a cool stare, she said, 'Totally.'

'Yeah, well, I don't seem to be having much luck in the dating department at the moment,' he muttered, his mind spinning back to the way he'd crashed and burned last night when he'd drunkenly attempted to chat up a woman at the bar. Not that his heart had really been in it.

She seemed to be studying him closely now, her eyes narrowed. 'Is that how you usually dress when you go out?' she asked after a beat.

'Yes,' he replied gruffly, guessing where this was going and trying not to grind his teeth.

'Maybe if you smartened yourself up a bit you'd

have more luck.' She waved her hand at his favourite T-shirt. 'I always find a new outfit and a haircut does my confidence the world of good.'

He dug his fingers into his thighs under the table. 'I happen to like the way I dress.'

She shot him a patronising smile. 'Well, I don't mean to be rude but your clothes look so old I suspect they're about to get a telegram from the Queen any day now.'

A heavy pulse had begun to throb in his head. 'Oh, really? Well, at least they have personality. You look like every other fashion victim on the street.'

She blinked at him in shock before regaining her composure. 'At least I made an effort with my appearance today,' she replied tightly, her words sounding more slurred now. 'It's clear you couldn't care less. You didn't even turn up on time to meet me, just left me sitting there like a lemon on my own for twenty minutes, only to turn up looking like a vagrant.'

He leaned forward in his chair, aware of his heart thumping hard against his chest, and matched her fierce gaze. 'Look, I get it. You feel some misplaced obligation to "take me in hand" and alleviate your guilt about not being there at the end for Amy.' He pointed a finger at her. 'But I don't need another sister figure and I certainly don't need some uptight do-gooder telling me how to live my life!'

'I'm only trying to help, Alex,' she snapped back.

'I don't need your help, Flora.'

'Is that right?'

'Yes!'

'Well, you know what? Since we're being so honest with each other now, perhaps you should know that Amy really struggled with your arrogant determination to keep everyone at arm's length,' she bit out, the increased volume of her voice causing the couple at the next table to turn and stare at them. She seemed to have hit her stride though, so didn't appear to notice. 'And it was incredibly frustrating for her that you found everything you did so easy when she had to work so hard for success. Then she had to watch while you just squandered your brain and your talents when she would have killed for them!' she hissed, her tongue obviously completely loosened now by strong cider and frustration.

Anger and guilt battled inside him. He was acutely aware of what a risk he'd taken, jacking in his steady job to follow his ambition to be a professional musician, but he didn't need to be reminded of it right now. 'I think what you really mean is that a slacker like me should have been the one to die, rather than my hard-working sister,' he bit out defensively.

'What? No!' She looked absolutely horrified that he could even suggest that.

He sighed, feeling his conscience prick, then held up a weary hand in recognition that he'd gone a bit too far with that statement. 'Okay, okay.' He took a steadying breath. 'Actually, I did know she felt like that—we talked about it before she died. But she told me to do what made me happy. She realised there was more to life than selling your soul just so you can wear overpriced designer clothes to eat at overhyped restaurants.'

Her eyes widened as if his words had hit her right in the solar plexus. 'So now you're having a go at me for enjoying the fruits of my success?'

He sighed in exasperation. 'No, that's not what I'm doing.' A voice in the back of his mind pointed out that it was exactly what he was doing.

'Well, it seems like it to me!' She took a deep, juddering breath. 'You know what? I'm going home. I know when I'm wasting my time.' Picking up her drink, she downed the rest of it, then stood up, wobbling a little on her heels. 'I was just trying to be friendly, Alex!' she said in a strangled voice. With that parting shot, she spun on the spot and stormed away from him, only just avoiding stumbling into the wall on her way to the door.

Alex dropped his head into his hands and cursed under his breath.

He really shouldn't have had a go at her like that, but when she'd started her character assassination of him something inside had snapped. He'd had just about enough of women telling him what was wrong with him.

The look of hurt on Flora's face had brought him up short though. Clearly she was still struggling to come to terms with his sister's sudden death and was desperately trying to find a way to give her life some meaning—by attempting to fix his.

Sighing, he got up from his chair and pulled his coat on. He couldn't just let her storm off in that state. He at least needed to make sure she got home safely, even if she refused to speak to him again.

After giving the barmaid a wave of thanks he followed Flora out of the pub. It was cold outside and he pulled his lapels across his throat and folded his arms against the icy wind as he trudged after her lone figure, watching in alarm as she swayed along the pavement, almost bumping into a couple coming the other way. He had no idea where she lived, but he hoped it wasn't far.

It wasn't.

She turned into the next street along, which housed a row of grand terraces, and strode up to a pillared entrance a few doors down. Fumbling in her handbag, she pulled out a key, which she proceeded to stab at the lock.

He watched her, half amused, half exasperated, as she failed to get the key into the lock over and over again. Shaking his head, he walked up behind her and took the key from her hand, feeling her jump in surprise at his unexpected presence.

'I don't need your help,' she said archly, but he ignored her, sliding the key into the lock and swinging the door open for her.

'After you,' he said, gesturing for her to go first, then rolling his eyes when she snatched the keys from his hand and swept past him with her head held high. This time, she managed to get the key to the inner flat into the lock on her second try. She barrelled inside, shrugging off her coat and haphazardly kicking off her shoes in the small but elegant hallway. Her whole posture was stiff now as if she was desperately trying to keep her composure under control and as he followed her inside the flat—just to make sure she wasn't going to walk into a wall and knock herself out—he saw her shoulders slump as if she'd lost the battle.

'Are you okay?' he asked quietly, worried that he'd gone too far in his anger and really upset her.

She turned back to look at him and his stomach dropped at the dejection he saw in her eyes.

'I'm sorry,' she said, surprising him with the genuine tone in her voice. He hadn't been expecting an apology.

'I've had such a terrible week. My boss doesn't trust me to do my job properly and you think I'm annoying and stuck-up.' She rubbed her hands over her eyes, smudging her make-up. 'I just wanted to do something good, Alex.'

'I know, I understand,' he said, moving towards her.

'I miss Amy so much.' Her voice broke on his sister's name and he swallowed in empathy.

'Don't you have other friends to talk to?' he asked gently.

'Yes, I have other friends! But I've grown apart from a lot of them since moving to the States and getting so swamped with work.' She flapped her hand in an overly dramatic gesture that gave away just how drunk she was. 'And anyway, none of them understand me the way that Amy did.'

Feeling out of his depth, he held up a hand, palm forward, to gesture for her to stay there. 'I'll get you a drink of water,' he said, backing away to find the kitchen. After locating a clean glass in the cupboard and filling it from a bottle of mineral water in the fridge, he returned to the living room to find her pacing up and down.

He held out the glass and she took it from him with a nod of thanks.

'She was always so good at giving it to me straight, then finding the perfect way to cheer me up,' she said, as if needing to get it all out now that she'd started talking about Amy. 'I need that.' She let out a big sigh, then looked at him beseechingly. 'Who's going to tell me to stop getting so wound up about nothing and "take a step back and breathe" now? Who's going to tease me about buying the exact same outfits year after year, whilst also complimenting me on my good taste? Or roll her eyes at my terrible jokes whilst also making me feel loved and respected? Who will ever understand me the way Amy did?' she finished on a whisper, her voice heavy with pain.

He had no idea how to make things better for her so, despite his frustration, he remained silent. It didn't seem as if Flora was really asking him for answers though. They both knew there weren't any right now.

She cocked her head to one side and gave him a smile that was full of anguish. 'We're never going to see her again, Alex. How can that possibly be? She was so young; she had so much to live for. I'll never see her cuddle the babies she wanted so desperately. She would have been such a good mother. I was going to be their favourite honorary aunt. It's such a waste of a good life. She had so much to offer the world. It's not fair. It's just not fair, Alex.'

'I know,' he said quietly, fighting back the swell of emotion he'd kept firmly under wraps since Amy had died. He had a horrible feeling if he let it go he'd lose himself completely.

Her eyes glimmered with tears as she looked at him, shaking her head.

'I hate the idea of moving through life without having any kind of a clue about what's lying in wait for me. When Amy was around I felt like I could cope with that fear because she'd always be there, at my back, ready to catch me. But I'm all alone now.' Sloshing water out of the glass with her drunken gesticulations, she put it down onto a side table next to her.

'Yeah, I know what you mean,' he said. And he did. It was something that terrified him too.

She put her head in her hands. 'Oh, God, I'm sorry. I must sound so selfish. I know I'm not the only person to lose someone, but that's how I feel when I wake up in the dark in the early hours—swamped with this cloying sense of dread and anger at the world.' She fisted her hands and shook them as if trying to throttle her emotions.

'Yeah, well, grief affects people in all sorts of ways.'

Looking back at him, she gazed right into his eyes, as if searching for something specific there.

'It doesn't seem to have affected you in the same way though. And I don't mean that as a criticism.' Her posture slumped now. 'I guess I'm just a weaker person than you.'

He moved towards her, putting his hand on her shoulder.

'I was lucky. I got to spend a lot of time with her at the end of her life,' he said quietly, realising now just how grateful he was to have had that opportunity.

'You see, that's the thing,' Flora said, then swallowed hard, as if forcing back her tears. 'I didn't get to say a proper goodbye and it's eating away at me. If only I'd booked my flight a day earlier. Twenty-four hours. That's all it would have taken to have been there to hug my best friend one last time.'

Her pain reached right inside him, twisting his guts. He drew her towards him, wrapping his arms around her and holding her tightly to him, at last feeling a real connection to her—that they were in this together.

She hugged him back with a fierceness that

nearly broke his heart, as if she was hoping that touching someone associated with Amy might bring back the peace she'd felt when his sister was around.

And then, as she drew back to look at him, the atmosphere switched in a second. Her pupils were blown in the dim light, making her eyes look huge. There was a strange expression in them now. Of longing. At least he was pretty sure that was what it was.

She raised her hand to his face and slid her fingertips along his jaw, frowning as they juddered across the bristles.

'You're a good person, Alex. Amy was so lucky to have you as a brother. I wish I had someone like you looking out for me.'

Before he realised what she was about to do, Flora lurched forwards and pressed her mouth against his, her lips warm and soft. The sweet scent of her invaded his senses as he stood there, stunned and rooted to the spot. His blood pounded hard through his veins as he fought off the strongest impulse just to let himself sink into the kiss.

But he knew he couldn't do that.

Carefully, reluctantly, he drew back from her, feeling her hands instinctively tighten around his back for a second before she realised he was deliberately pulling away.

'That's a really bad idea, Flora. One I think you'll regret in the morning when you're stone-cold sober.'

She shook her head, looking a little bewildered. 'I won't—'

But he wasn't prepared to argue this with her when she was drunk and hurting. 'Come on, it's time for you to go to bed.'

Her shoulders slumped as if all her energy had drained away now and she meekly allowed him to lead her out of the living room and into what he correctly surmised was her bedroom.

'Just sleep it off, okay? Things will seem a bit better in the morning. We just need to take each day as it comes.'

She nodded, then yawned loudly. 'I'm so tired,' she murmured.

'I can tell,' he said, pulling back the duvet so she could crawl into bed, still wearing her clothes. He figured it was probably better to leave her like that than attempt to undress her—that could only lead to more misunderstandings. Once she was settled, he pulled the duvet over her and went to fetch her glass of water from the living room. By the time he returned with it she seemed to be asleep already, her breathing soft and regular in the quiet of the room.

He watched her for a moment, just to make sure she really was asleep, feeling a sudden swell of compassion for her. Shaking off the weird twitch of nerves this produced, he crept out of the room, letting out a big yawn of his own. His insomnia seemed to have well and truly caught up with him today. Moving over to the sofa, he lay down, pulling a blanket he found neatly folded on the arm over his body.

He'd stay here for an hour or so, just to make sure she wasn't ill. He knew how evil that local cider was—he'd been caught out by it himself before.

Shifting onto his side, he felt the waistband of his jeans dig in to him, so undid them and shucked them off. Yes, that was much more comfortable. Though he was pretty hot now. She seemed to have her heating turned up to full. He tugged his T-shirt off too, feeling relief at the sensation of cooler air on his hot skin. His whole body felt overstimulated after the kiss she'd planted on his mouth.

Pushing the memory far out of his head, he let out a deep sigh to expel the tension. After the soul-crushing end to his relationship with Tia, the very last thing he needed right now was to get caught up in something new. He had a strong suspicion, from what he'd seen of Flora so far, that someone as intense and focused as her would be the kind of woman who would want to go all in on a relationship too. He needed to look after himself right now, so there was no space for anyone else in his life.

Fluffing up the cushion, he flopped back down

and let out a groan of tiredness. There, that was better. He'd just close his eyes for a minute, then get out of there once he was sure she'd be okay on her own.

CHAPTER THREE

BRIGHT WINTRY SUNLIGHT playing against his eyelids woke Alex up from a deep sleep. Peeling his lids open he looked around him, wondering where the heck he'd woken up. He didn't recognise the cornice on the ceiling or the glass chandelier hanging from it. Turning his head, he looked around the room to find he was lying on a large red velvet sofa, surrounded by expensive-looking antique furniture. There was a large Christmas tree in the bay window adorned with tasteful decorations and sprigs of holly jauntily arranged in an elegant vase on the mantelpiece. Well, this definitely wasn't his place.

Then it all came rushing back to him. He was still at Flora's flat.

Sitting up, he rubbed his hand over his skull, attempting to get the blood flowing to his brain.

He'd not meant to stay all night, but her sofa had been so comfortable he hadn't woken up after the two-hour stretch he usually managed these days.

His mouth felt as if someone had rubbed it with sandpaper. Too much beer again last night. Swinging his legs off the sofa, he stood up and stretched, feeling the air on his sleep-warmed skin. He'd grab a quick drink of water, then get dressed and out of there. She didn't need to know he'd stayed the whole night.

As he moved towards the doorway his gaze caught on a framed photo on the sideboard. Stopping to pick it up, he examined the picture of Flora and his sister, arms flung around each other, smiling at the camera. They both had deep, healthy-looking tans and sunglasses pushed jauntily back on their heads. They looked so carefree it made something tighten uncomfortably inside him. The photo must have been taken during one of the summer holidays to Greece or Italy or France that they'd taken together each year. Something Amy had loved doing.

The sight of his sister looking so happy brought

a lump to his throat. He thought about what Flora had said last night about how unfair it was that Amy's life had been cut so cruelly short. She'd died before she'd had time to do all the things she'd wanted to do. Particularly have a family of her own.

He'd never really been that interested in having kids himself, but Amy had wanted them desperately ever since they were little. It had probably been something to do with not feeling as if their own family was as complete and functional as it should have been, what with their father running off to Thailand when they were six and never getting into contact with them again. Their mum had been a trooper, giving them every material thing they'd ever needed, but he knew how hard it had been for her on her own. She hadn't always had the patience or the time to give him and Amy the hugs and love they'd craved. Or perhaps it had been down to her having a broken heart, which had failed her when she was only forty-seven, leaving them parentless aged nineteen.

At least he and Amy had had each other to lean on.

Not wanting to dwell any longer on that thought, he put the photo back with a trembling hand. There was a gasp of surprise behind him and he twisted round to see Flora standing there, blearily rubbing the sleep out of her eyes.

'Alex!' she said, her eyes widening as she ran her gaze up and down his nearly naked body. *At least I left my boxer shorts on*, he thought wryly, taking in the thunderstruck expression on her face.

She slumped against the door frame, as if needing it to hold her up. *Hangover*, he thought, though he didn't say it. He didn't think she'd appreciate him pointing out the obvious right then. She'd changed out of yesterday's clothes and was now wearing a blindingly white fluffy bathrobe. He guessed she hadn't looked in the mirror yet though because she had panda eyes from her smudged make-up and her hair was a mess. She looked like a completely different person from the polished perfectionist of yesterday. He actually found her much more attractive like that, rumpled and sexy, not that he was going to admit it out loud.

'What are you doing here?' Her eyes widened even more as a thought seemed to strike her. 'Oh, God, we didn't—?'

Her hands flew to her face. 'Oh, no, we *didn't*, did we?'

He shook his head, riled by her over-the-top alarm. 'No. We didn't. You tried to kiss me, and I stopped you. You passed out on your bed— alone—and I slept on your sofa.'

'I tried to *kiss* you?' She looked even more horrified by this. 'Oh, God, I must have been really drunk.'

'Gee, thanks.'

She flushed and held up an apologetic hand. 'I just mean I wouldn't normally do something like that. You're a lovely guy, but I think we can safely say we'd never naturally date. We'd make a very odd couple.'

'Very odd,' he said, though he felt a strange reluctance about agreeing with her. They weren't that dissimilar, not really. His sister never would have been friends with Flora if she hadn't seen the good in her.

Not that he was interested in her in a romantic way, of course. The way he'd instinctively responded to her when she'd kissed him had been a shock, sure, but she was right—they would never work as a couple. He'd only reacted like that because he'd been missing human contact recently.

'Hey, speaking of dating,' Flora went on, pulling her robe more tightly around her body, 'I meant to say last night—before I messed up by being really rude to you about your clothes and—' she paused as a sheepish look flashed across her face '—the other things.' She produced a strange sort of grimacing grin, clearly hoping that would suffice as an apology.

'I have a friend who lives just outside Bath. I think you'd really get on with her,' she went on quickly before he could get a word in. 'She's big into music—she plays the harp, I think.' She flapped her hand as if annoyed with her less than perfect memory. 'Anyway, I met up with her for a coffee the other day—we hadn't seen each other since school—and she's single at the moment. I mentioned you to her and she seemed really interested in meeting you.'

His heart sank. 'You're trying to set me up on a blind date?'

'Sure, why not? Isn't that how most people meet their partners these days? Internet dating or through a friend of a friend?'

'I don't think so, Flora.'

Folding her arms, she fixed him with a concerned stare. 'Well, I think you should put yourself out there again. Didn't you say yesterday that you'd promised Amy you'd get on with your life and not mope about?'

She looked so expectant now he couldn't bear to refute it. Maybe if he agreed to go along with this nonsense she'd feel that she'd fulfilled her duty to Amy and leave him the heck alone.

Sighing, he nodded wearily in agreement. 'Okay. Fine. I'll meet her.'

'Really?' she asked, as if she thought she'd imagined him agreeing to it.

'Yes, really. Just don't expect to hear wedding bells any time soon. I'm not up for anything serious at the moment.'

'Sure, sure, that's fine,' she said, but he could tell from the gleam in her eye that she was hoping they'd hit it off.

God help him.

Flora tried not to think about how she'd kissed Alex.

She tried not to think about it at work when she was supposed to be leading a meeting and at home when she was heating up a meal for one from the freezer. She definitely tried not to think about it when she was lying in bed finding it hard to sleep.

She'd pretended to Alex that she didn't remember doing it. But she did. It had been wonderful to be held like that: to feel so close to him. He'd smelled of spicy aftershave and leather and comfort, and it had made her heart flutter to feel that connection with him.

Obviously drinking cider on an empty stomach had been to blame for her uncharacteristic slip-up, but she was also unnervingly aware that it had seemed like exactly the right thing to do at the time. Perhaps in her drunken haze she'd thought they could comfort each other or something. She realised now what a crazy idea that had been, but at the time it had seemed so simple and logical.

In the cold light of day she didn't think for a second they should actually do something like that though. As she'd pointed out whilst desperately trying to keep her cool in the face of his half nakedness and hide her discomfort at him seeing her in such a bedraggled, bed-headed state, they'd make a very peculiar couple indeed.

It wasn't that she couldn't see what women found attractive about him. She wasn't blind—she appreciated his square-jawed handsomeness and ultramasculine, hard-muscled body—something that a slovenly musician who spent most of his time drinking beer in the pub had no right to have. But she really didn't see him like that. Like a potential partner. He was just Amy's scruffy, work-shy brother.

No. Her friend Lucy was a much better fit for him. They both had a love of music in common after all. And if he and Lucy hit it off, she'd be able to go back to New York with a clear conscience, knowing that someone who lived nearby was looking out for him. Even if the two of them only became friends she'd be able to check with Lucy about how he was doing. She certainly didn't expect Alex to tell her the truth over the phone, based on his reluctance to discuss his feelings last night.

She was determined not to regret the kiss they'd shared though. Why should she? It had been acknowledged as an aberration and they'd moved on from it. And she'd learnt an important lesson—no more of the local cider for her. It seemed as though that stuff was her 'life event catalyst' as Alex had called it, and she preferred not to put herself in such a vulnerable position again, especially in front of Alex. Although, to give him his due, he had been incredibly kind to her, making sure she got safely home and even sleeping on the sofa to keep an eye on her. She was grateful for that. He'd been a gentleman about it too. He hadn't teased her about her imprudent drunken behaviour and had even agreed to a date with Lucy before making a quick exit that morning.

So things were looking up.

She just needed to keep her fingers crossed that he and Lucy got on.

With that in mind, she'd put in a call to her friend as soon as Alex had left. Lucy had been delighted with the idea of meeting him the following Friday night.

Tonight, in fact.

Flora checked her watch for the umpteenth time, wondering what the two of them were doing right now as she lay on her sofa half watching an old film and half working on her laptop. Lucy had suggested meeting Alex at a local bar on the edge of the city, so it was unlikely she'd bump into them if she wandered into town. Not that she was going to do that.

She jumped as her phone made a loud beeping noise to signal a text arriving. Scooping it up from the arm of the sofa, she was a little alarmed to see it was from Alex. It was only eight-forty. Wasn't he supposed to be on a date right now?

We met. It went fine. I hope you're happy. Alex.

Fine? Fine! He thought that 'fine' was a good enough result, did he? Scrolling through to his number in her contacts, she pressed the icon to connect them and waited impatiently for him to pick up. It took five rings before he finally answered with a curt, 'Hello, Flora.'

'What do you mean, "It went fine"? What went wrong?'

'Nothing went wrong. It was a nice evening. She seems…nice.'

'Ugh. "Nice" is even worse than "fine".'

'What do you want me to say? That we're engaged and getting married next week?'

She caught her huff of breath just in time. 'No, of course not. I was just hoping you'd make a bit of an effort.'

There was a short silence before he spoke. 'How do you know I didn't make an effort?'

'Just a hunch,' she muttered in frustration.

'Well, I did, Flora. I listened to all her stories about her ex-boyfriend and all the awful things he'd done to her and how he was still in contact with her and should she speak to him or just ignore him. It seemed to me that she needed a relationship counsellor, not a date.'

Flora closed her eyes and bit back a sigh of defeat. 'Damn. Okay. Maybe I miscalculated. I thought it seemed like she was ready to start dating again.'

'You knew about the recent ex?' His voice was heavy with accusation, as if he thought she'd deliberately set him up with a no-hoper.

Flora felt her face heat. 'She mentioned him a couple of times, yes, but I thought it would be fine.'

Fine. There was that word again.

His sigh of annoyance sent a shiver of guilt through her. 'Look, I thought the best thing for her would be to get out and meet someone new.

To be honest, her ex sounded like a bit of a loony to me.'

'That's great, Flora. So now I need to look over my shoulder in case her stalker ex is on my tail looking for retribution because I went out on a date with his woman.'

'Don't be ridiculous. That won't happen,' she cajoled.

'It'd better not,' he growled back.

There was a tense pause where they both breathed heavily down the line.

'Okay, look, I'm sorry,' she said, sighing. Deep down, she knew that it had probably been a crazy idea all along. She'd wanted to be able to fix this easily and she'd got a bit carried away. But this was Alex's heart she was trying to shore up, not a flagging brand of soft drinks.

'It was a stupid idea. Of course you're not going to want to embark on a new relationship so soon after everything that's happened to you recently. I just wanted to do something to try to help in some way.'

There was another loaded pause before he

spoke. 'It's okay. I appreciate the sentiment behind it. But can we please agree right now that you won't attempt any more matchmaking?' He let out a gentle snort. 'It seems we've found the one thing you're not very good at.'

Pushing away the perplexity this comment provoked, she forced herself to laugh. 'Yeah, I promise I'll keep those urges to myself from now on.'

'Probably best.'

She sank back onto the sofa, grateful that at least he wasn't angry with her any more. 'So what are you going to do with the rest of your evening?' she asked tentatively.

'I thought I'd go for a swim to clear my head,' he said, sounding fed up.

'Where are you going? Is there a good pool near here?'

'I usually use the one at the Thermal Spa. It's closest to my flat and there's a heated outdoor pool on the roof.'

'Ooh, I've heard about that but I've not had chance to go yet.'

'It's great, you should check it out some time.'

'Maybe I should come with you now,' she blurted out. She really didn't want him to be alone when he was in such a bad mood. He'd probably go home afterwards and drink too much whisky again and she didn't like the thought of him doing that. Not on her watch.

There was a pause. 'Uh…okay, if you like.' He sounded as if he was really hoping that she was joking.

'Great,' she said assertively, ignoring his reticence.

She'd not put on a swimming costume in a very long time. Swimming always seemed such a lot of hassle for so little gain, what with having to wash and blow-dry her hair and apply make-up twice in one day—but this was for a good cause. He might not think that he needed her right now, and he clearly wasn't ready to date again, but she wasn't giving up on her promise to Amy to look out for him.

'Okay, I'll meet you there in ten minutes,' he said gruffly.

'What? Why so soon?' she asked, a little panicked about the lack of time to get herself organised.

'It closes at ten so we'll need to be there for the last session at nine o'clock.'

'Ah. Okay. In that case I'll see you there in ten minutes,' she said.

'Great,' he replied, not sounding like he genuinely thought it was, before cutting the call.

She had a moment of panic when she realised that she didn't have a swimming costume here in Bath, but after a quick bit of online research she discovered that a few of the clothes shops were open late for Christmas shopping.

Luckily it was only a five-minute dash from her flat into town so she was able to run into one of the stores and grab a swimming costume in her size from the sale rack, before dodging her way through the still-heavy crowd of shoppers to the Thermal Spa. She spotted Alex waiting for her outside the glass-fronted entrance with a rolled-up towel tucked under his arm.

Alex waved to Flora as she dashed towards him with an expensive-looking tote bag slung over her shoulder, wondering again how he'd found himself meeting her here tonight.

After it had become obvious that he and Lucy weren't going to hit it off, he'd made up an excuse about a rehearsal and legged it out of there as fast as he could. He'd been intent on sinking a couple of beers he had in the fridge at home when it occurred to him that Lucy might call Flora to tell her how he'd disappeared on her and he'd decided it would be best to head her off at the pass.

Mistakenly, it seemed, he'd chosen an activity he thought Flora would never be interested in when she'd asked him what he was planning to do with the rest of his evening. He'd not banked on her determination to maintain control over the situation.

It was obvious now that she had made it her mission to stick to him like glue and he wasn't going to be given any choice in the matter.

Once they'd got through the short queue at the spa they went their separate ways at the communal changing rooms, arranging to meet at the pool on the roof. Alex had already been swimming for ten minutes in the warm water, with the cold air stinging his cheeks, when Flora finally made an appearance. The complimentary robe was wrapped tightly around her and her hair was tied in an elegant topknot.

He gave her a somewhat reluctant wave, hoping that she'd choose not to brave the cold out here and swim in the indoor pool instead. She spotted him and waved back, a little mechanically he thought, and shuffled towards the cubbyholes provided to stash robes and slippers.

As she turned back to survey the pool he saw apprehension flash in her eyes. He guessed that she was determined to hang out with him, but the thought of doing it semi-naked didn't massively appeal.

Well, she was the one who had insisted on coming with him.

His eyes widened and his pulse stuttered as he watched her slide off her robe to uncover the most revealing swimming costume he'd ever seen in his life. The material was cut high on her hips, forming a deep V that barely covered her modesty. The same went for the top of the costume, which was cut so low the flash of skin down her chest stopped just above her belly button. He found he was having a hard time tearing his eyes away from the gentle swell of her breasts, which were barely covered by the tight material.

From the look of trepidation on her face she wasn't entirely comfortable wearing it. Not that it had stopped her from coming out in public in it.

The woman certainly had guts.

His mouth suddenly felt inexplicably dry as he watched her saunter down the steps into the pool, keeping her head held high, despite the flush of colour that stained her neck and cheeks. Once fully immersed, she swam towards him with a lofty look on her face, appearing less embarrassed now that her body was hidden under the water.

'Nice cossie,' he quipped, finding it impossible not to tease her and biting back a grin as he watched the colour return to her cheeks.

'I didn't bring one to England with me so I only

bought it five minutes ago. It didn't look like it'd be so revealing in the shop,' she shot back.

He couldn't help but laugh at the odd mix of superiority and mortification on her face.

'Well, you can pull it off,' he reassured her, feeling the urge to be kind now. And it wasn't as if he was lying either. She had an incredible body—curvy but toned, as if she ate healthily and spent plenty of time exercising.

'Er…thanks,' she said, looking a bit shocked at the compliment and a little unsure about how to react to it. She must have decided that he was still teasing her because she swam away without another word, over to the other side of the pool where there were benches under the water and jets making bubbles like a hot tub.

Shrugging off her abandonment of him, Alex did laps of the pool, dodging around the few other people courageous enough to venture up there in the dead of winter. The water was wonderfully warm once you were in it, but he knew from experience it took a brave soul to get out afterwards with the cold wind whistling across your damp skin.

Once he'd got rid of the weird rush of adrenaline the sight of Flora in that swimming costume had brought on, he swam over to where she was crouching under a small waterfall. He watched as she moved from side to side, letting the strong jet of water massage her shoulders. Her make-up had begun to run down her face, but he thought that if he pointed it out he'd probably get dunked for his trouble.

'How's that working out for you?' he asked once she'd opened her eyes and noticed him there.

'It's absolute bliss,' she moaned in a voice so full of pleasure it made his stomach do a weird kind of flip.

'Here, come under—it's great,' she said, moving to one side to give him room to experience it too. She was right—it was wonderful to feel the water pounding hard on his shoulders, pummelling away the tension from the last few days. He closed his eyes and let himself feel the pleasure of it, allowing his thoughts to drift away to nothingness, a state that was rather alien to him at the moment. It had been a long time since his head had been clear of swirling chaos.

When he opened his eyes, Flora was staring at him with a strange expression on her face, as if trying to figure out what was going through his mind.

'How was your week? Did rehearsals go well?' she asked, glancing away to watch her hands as she swished them through the water in front of her.

His mood dimmed at the memory of what a joke his musical skills had been this past week.

'They went okay,' he muttered.

'Oh, dear.'

She looked back at him with sympathy in her eyes and on the spur of the moment he decided to trust her with the problems he was having. Perhaps talking about it would actually help. 'To be honest, I'm finding it hard to feel the joy in playing at the moment,' he said with a sigh.

She gave a sage sort of nod. 'Well, that's not entirely surprising; grief can knock the stuffing right out of you.' Bouncing gently on her toes, she flashed him an empathetic smile. 'I'm sure your muse will come back soon enough. You just need to work through this rough patch,' she stated with an authority that made him suspect she'd been telling herself the same thing.

He continued to look at her for a moment, and it suddenly occurred to him that she was the only person in the world who knew exactly how he was feeling right now.

She gazed back at him, the intensity in her eyes doing strange things to his insides.

'Hey, have you lain on your back and looked at the sky yet?' he asked, to break the unnerving mood that had fallen between them.

'Uh…no,' she said, looking a little discombobulated by the sudden change in subject.

He waved for her to follow him. 'Come on, it's really worth it. You can actually see some of the stars, despite the light pollution.'

They floated on their backs, side by side, staring up at the velvety midnight-blue sky, pointing out the star clusters that twinkled faintly above them.

'This reminds me of the holiday to the south of France I went on with Amy a couple of years ago,' Flora said, lifting her head out of the water to look at him. 'We were staying at this gorgeous little *gîte* near St Tropez and we spent most of the week floating around in the outdoor pool because it was so hot.' She smiled, the look in her eyes faraway but happy. 'One night we got so drunk Amy fell over a small wall in the garden and didn't realise she'd broken her toe until the next morning.'

'I remember her telling me about that,' Alex said with a grin.

'It was so swollen she couldn't wear anything but flip-flops for a couple of weeks afterwards.' Flora smiled widely. 'Unfortunately the English weather wasn't as clement as it had been in France, so she looked completely ridiculous walking around in the pouring rain with her feet bare and pink from the cold.'

She giggled at the memory, the sound of it making something fizz in his belly.

'She didn't complain though,' Flora continued. 'She never complained about anything. Just got on with it.' He could hear in her voice how much she'd loved his sister and he suddenly understood what had drawn Amy to her. She was clearly a fiercely loyal friend once you got past her hard shell.

'Yeah, she was a trouper all right,' Alex said, thinking back to how his sister had remained her cheery, positive self even during her last week in the hospice. 'She was telling jokes right up until the end of her life,' he said, swallowing a hard lump that had formed in his throat.

They talked for a while longer as they floated around in the water, about memories they had of Amy and all the times she'd cracked a joke, even though the situation had seemed desperate to everyone else. She'd always had a way of seeing light in the dark.

It was wonderful to conjure up memories of his sister like this and hear things he'd never known about her too. Having always been so wrapped up in his music he'd not paid as much attention to what was going on in Amy's life as perhaps he should have done. He knew that. Flora had been bang on when she'd accused him of keeping people at arm's length. He did do that. So hearing about a previously unknown side of Amy's life from her best friend made him feel closer to his sister.

The whole experience was so enriching that Alex felt the first lift of positivity for the future he'd had in months. So it was with regret that he dropped his feet back to the floor and stood up, aware of Flora doing the same next to him.

'I guess we should get out before they close the place,' she said, tugging on the straps of her swimming costume and looking a little uncomfortable about the idea of leaving the refuge of the water.

'Yeah, I guess so.' They looked at each other for a moment and he was aware that a subtle shift had occurred in their relationship. 'I tell you what,' he said, motioning for Flora to stay where she was. 'Wait there a minute.' After swimming to the steps he hauled himself out of the water into the freezing air and moved briskly to the cubbyholes to grab her robe. He held it open at the edge of the pool, averting his gaze so he was staring out over at the view of the cityscape instead of directly at her. He heard her wade quickly out of the water and as soon as he felt she was close enough he wrapped the robe around her, hiding her from any prying eyes.

'Thanks,' she said, looking up into his face and giving him a smile of genuine humility.

'You're welcome,' he replied, taking a step back from her. He had the strangest compulsion to tie the belt tightly around the gown for her to make sure her modesty remained intact, but he stopped himself from reaching towards her. He wasn't sure whether she'd appreciate such an intimate and domineering gesture coming from him.

They stood there for a moment, smiling at each other, before Flora broke the moment by gesturing towards the steps that led back down to the changing rooms.

'Okay, well, I'll see you at the front desk. Unless you want to get going straight away?' she said, clearly trying to sound unbothered either way.

'No, I'll wait for you. See you there in a few minutes,' he said, not wanting to end their night together just yet. Not when they were finally starting to find common ground.

In actual fact, he had to wait a while longer than he'd anticipated at the front desk before Flora appeared with her hair blow-dried back to perfection but her face free of the heavy make-up she'd been wearing earlier.

She looked younger and more approachable like that and it triggered instinctive warmth towards her that hadn't been there previously. She wasn't such a bad person to hang out with, he mused, and it was actually great to be able to talk to someone else who knew Amy well. None of his friends here in Bath had even met his sister. She'd cited being too busy at her job up in Glasgow to make it down south to see him when he'd first moved here, and then of course she'd become too ill to travel.

'Sorry to keep you,' Flora said as she reached him, not quite meeting his gaze.

'No problem,' he said. 'I barely recognised you. You look different without all that make-up on,' he joked.

She shot him a startled frown.

'In a good way, I mean,' he said quickly. 'I prefer you without it. You really don't need it.' He shrugged. 'I always think the natural look is sexier on a woman.'

For the first time since he'd met her she looked a little uncertain about what to say next.

'I guess I'd better let you get home,' she said after a beat, giving him a tight smile and making a move towards the exit. He followed her, noticing how stiff her posture seemed again now.

'You're welcome to come back to my place for a drink,' he said, realising that he didn't want to be on his own right now.

She turned to give him a look of surprise. Evidently she'd been expecting him to stride off without even a backwards glance. His stomach did a flip at the pleasure on her face.

'That would be great, if you're sure you're not too tired?'

'Exhaustion seems to be my permanent state of being at the moment,' he joked. 'But seriously, you're most welcome,' he added when he saw her face fall a little.

'Well, okay then,' she said, recovering quickly. 'Lead the way.'

CHAPTER FOUR

ALEX LET THEM into his ground floor flat, which was housed in one of the elegant golden stone-fronted Georgian terraces that the city was so famous for, and gave a wry smile at the look of shock and disorientation on Flora's face as she realised he hadn't led her into a hovel of iniquity.

'This is—' She gazed around at the high-ceilinged room, taking in the squashy leather sofas and the sharply designed high-quality furniture he'd collected throughout his year of living here. His pride and joy, a black lacquered grand piano, stood proudly in the bay window, while his other instruments—a guitar, zither and accordion as well as various other accompaniments—leaned neatly against the wall next to it.

'—quite something,' she finished, turning to

give him an earnest smile. It seemed that he'd finally been able to impress her.

'Thanks. I bought the place as soon as I moved here from London.'

She nodded slowly, her eyes narrowing in thought. 'You used your half of the money your mum left you from the sale of her house in Richmond.'

He grimaced to himself, realising there could be other moments like this, where she told him things about himself that he had no idea she knew. Of course Amy had always been a blabbermouth and was bound to have talked about him, but the realisation that she knew him much better than he'd realised made him a little nervous.

'I made a lot of money when I was working in corporate finance in my early twenties and made some sound investments, so I'm in a pretty good financial position now. I give piano lessons too, though I mostly do cut-price deals for people who wouldn't normally be able to afford them.'

'Not just a pretty face then,' she said, then looked pained as if embarrassed by blurting that out.

'Would you like a drink?' he asked, shaking off his sudden discomposure and moving towards the door that led through to the small kitchen at the back of the flat.

'Do you have peppermint tea?'

He turned back to fix her with a look of disgust. 'No. I don't drink that muck.'

She frowned. 'Fruit tea?' she asked hopefully.

'Nope.'

'Anything without caffeine?' she asked with a small sigh of exasperation.

'No. I have coffee or builder's tea.'

'I'll take a glass of water. Mineral if you've got it.'

'Tap water it is,' he said, smiling as he turned away from her comical eye-roll to stride away to the kitchen.

When he returned a few minutes later with a mug of strong coffee for himself and a pint of tap water for her, she was drumming her fingertips on the arm of the sofa while her gaze darted around the room.

If he didn't know better he'd think she was nervous about being here with him. But why would she be? Apparently she knew him better than he knew himself.

He put the tray down on the coffee table before sitting on the sofa next to her. She flashed him a smile of thanks and reached for the water, taking a delicate sip before replacing it on the table.

Why was the atmosphere suddenly so awkward? he wondered as he sipped at his scalding coffee.

Perhaps because they were letting each other get closer and it was a bit unnerving. After all, she was his sister's best friend and under any other circumstances they'd probably never have crossed each other's paths. He was glad he'd met her out tonight though. It felt like a small but significant development in his life.

'So Lucy told me you weren't always the polished paragon of fashion I see before me today,' he said in an attempt to lighten the atmosphere, gesturing to the designer outfit she'd worn to the swimming pool.

Was he imagining it, or had her face paled a

little? She certainly looked a bit self-conscious all of a sudden as she raised her hands and surreptitiously ran her forefingers over her perfectly arched eyebrows.

'Oh, really? What exactly did she say?' she asked in what was clearly intended to be a nonchalant tone but fell well short of the mark. At least it came across that way to him.

He didn't want to make her uncomfortable, so he shrugged and said, 'Just that you were a bit of a rock chick when you were younger.'

'Yes, well, we all have our ridiculous phases. I had a thing for musician types for a while, but it never suited me.' Her back was ramrod straight now. 'Is that all she told you about me?'

'Yes, even though I tried to get all the dirt on you I could,' he joked, wondering what her uneasiness was all about. Didn't everyone have embarrassing clothing faux pas in their past?

'Well, I was pretty boring apart from that,' she said tonelessly, not playing along with his jokey manner, which made him suspect there was more to this than she was willing to admit. He had a gut feeling that if he dug deeper he'd discover something a little more painful in her past.

'You know, I can't picture you as a child,' he said, flashing her a playful grin, hoping to lift her mood. 'You're such a grown-up.'

She raised a reproachful eyebrow, but he could tell from the smile in her eyes that she'd taken his teasing as a joke this time. 'Somehow I don't think you mean that as a compliment.'

He just grinned back.

Getting up from the sofa, she walked towards his piano and sat down on the stool, gently pressing a couple of the keys.

'Do you play?' he asked, nodding towards the instrument that had given him so much pleasure in his life. The day he'd bought that piano had been the happiest of his life.

'No.' She shook her head. 'I took some lessons when I was younger, but—' She paused, as if pulling herself back from the brink of saying something a little too revealing.

'But?' he prompted, getting up from the sofa

and joining her, fascinated to hear what she'd say next.

Clearing her throat, she gave a little shrug. 'It never really stuck with me. My sister got all the creative and musical genes. According to her, I'm completely tone-deaf.'

'That's a shame,' he said, sensing there was more to this story than she was giving up.

'I know, right? And I have the perfect hands for playing the piano.' She held her hands up, spanning her long fingers to show him. 'Piano player's hands, or so I've been told.'

'It's not too late to give it another go,' he pointed out.

Her returning smile was tight. 'I don't have time for anything outside of work at the moment. It's pretty intensive, especially with the commute on top.'

A question about why she'd chosen to live in Bath and commute all the way into London was on the tip of his tongue, but he stopped himself from asking it at the last moment. He didn't really want to get into a boring conversation about train delays and ticket prices.

In fact, he'd rather not think about London and the life he'd moved away from at all.

'Hey, what are you doing for Christmas?' she asked, breaking into his unsettling train of thought.

'Er...' He had to think fast. No way was he admitting that he was planning to spend it alone getting slowly sozzled in front of the TV. It was a matter of pride. And he didn't want her thinking she had to invite him to do something with her either. 'I'm getting together with my bandmates. None of us have family nearby so we're all going for a pub Christmas lunch.'

This answer seemed to please her because she gave him a bright smile. 'Oh, good. I was afraid you might be on your own. I'd have invited you to spend it with me, but I promised my parents I'd go up to Derbyshire to see them this year.'

He wondered why this had produced a pinched little scowl on her face.

'I'm glad you've got somewhere to go,' he said,

pushing away his concern. Perhaps her family got up each other's noses when they got together over Christmas. He leaned back against the side of the piano and smiled down at her. 'I bet your parents will be pleased to see you. Amy mentioned that you've not been back to England since moving to the States.'

Her cheeks flushed with colour. 'No, well, it's so expensive to fly over, and my boss is pretty strict about how much holiday we can take.'

She got up from the piano stool as if wanting to call a halt to this particular conversation and gave what he could have sworn was a fake yawn. 'Anyway, I'd better get home. It's getting late and I'm exhausted after that swim.'

He pushed away from the piano and straightened up too. 'Sure. Well, thanks for keeping me company.'

Making her way towards the door, she turned back to give him a friendly smile. 'No problem. It was fun.'

He had a sudden urge to make some sort of a

gesture to show her he really did appreciate the effort she was making to get to know him.

'Hey, guess what?' he said, following her into the hallway.

'What?' she asked, turning back from opening the door to look at him expectantly.

'I managed to get a spare ticket to my gig next weekend. If you're free, it'd be great if you could come.' He held up both hands. 'No pressure though.'

The delighted smile she gave him made his insides heat.

'Sure, I'd love to, if you really want me to come?' From the wobble in her voice he suspected she thought he might just be offering it to be magnanimous. Which wasn't the case. He really did want her to come and support him. It would actually be pretty great to have someone there just for him.

Sighing, he rubbed a hand over his face. 'Look, I'm sorry if I gave you the impression I wasn't interested in being friends the other night. It's just that my head's been full of this gig and there hasn't been much room for anything else in there.' He tapped the side of his head with two fingers and grinned at her.

She smiled back, her eyes soft with understanding.

His stomach did a weird flip.

'It's fine, I get it.'

'And I appreciate you making the effort to arrange a date with Lucy for me, even if we didn't hit it off,' he added with a wry grimace.

She flashed him a shamefaced smile, then swung the door open and exited into the cold night air.

He was just about to shut the door behind her when she turned back and said, 'Thanks for letting me come with you tonight. I had fun.' And with one last sincere smile, she went striding off down the street.

He stared after her, his insides feeling a little churned up, stunned to acknowledge that, despite all his expectations to the contrary, he'd had fun tonight too.

* * *

Flora spent the next week battling with her boss to give her the autonomy she needed to do her job properly. It was only the thought of seeing Alex again at the weekend that kept her from a complete and utter meltdown at the end of each day.

While the thought of sitting through a couple of hours of jazz didn't exactly appeal, she was actually quite glad to be getting out and social-ising on a Saturday night. When she was on her own she had a tendency to go over and over the issues from her working week and it always sent her into a downward spiral of anxiety—a men-tal state she'd struggled with on and off all her working life. It had been worth putting up with for the kudos of the position and the generous pay packet her job offered, but sometimes she felt desperate for a reprieve from it. At times like those, she imagined how great it would feel to be her own boss—primarily for the enhanced sense of control it would offer.

Their jaunt to the swimming pool and the subsequent softening in Alex's attitude towards her had left her feeling much more positive about being able to fulfil Amy's last wish though. To her surprise, she'd found herself actually enjoying his company. He wasn't such a bad person to hang out with once you got past the glib flippancy and the tendency to flirt with anything that moved. His comment about her looking good without her make-up had surprised her too. It had been a long time since she'd gone out in public without a full face of make-up, but in her haste to meet him there on time she'd forgotten to put any in her bag. His kind words had given her shaky confidence a much-needed boost.

Saturday finally came around and, keeping his comments in mind, she kept her make-up light and chose her outfit carefully. She didn't want to stand out like a sore thumb, she told herself as she pulled on a pair of boot-cut jeans and a cashmere jumper in a beautiful sapphire blue that she hadn't been able to resist buying that morning.

It wasn't as if they were going out on a date—it was just one friend supporting another—but she wanted to look as if she'd made a bit of an effort.

After pulling on her high-heeled boots and sliding her arms into her long, satisfyingly heavy woollen trench coat, she let herself out of her flat and set off towards the venue where the gig was happening on the other side of the city.

Bath's centre was so small it only took her around fifteen minutes to reach her destination, so she walked through the doors of the old converted railway station where the gig was being held a few minutes earlier than she'd planned. While she hated unpunctuality, she also feared turning up too early for things, then having to hang around on her own like a saddo before they started. Thank goodness for being able to hide behind the safety of a mobile phone these days, she thought as she stepped through the door of the mostly empty venue.

And what a gorgeous venue it was.

It was as if she'd stepped back into the early nineteen-thirties.

The whole place was done out in the art deco style, with the sharply defined geometric motif of a sunrise decorating the large steel and glass bar at the back of the room and the long mirrored wall behind it reflecting a mind-boggling array of colourful spirit bottles. Groups of black lacquered tables and chairs, decorated with holly and silver stars in a nod to the Christmas season, faced the long, low stage at the other end of the room where the band's instruments were set up. To the left of the stage, strung with glinting white fairy lights, sat a black, highly polished upright piano.

And sitting on the stool in front of it, looking intently at a sheaf of sheet music, was Alex.

Except he hardly looked like the man she'd got to know over the last few weeks. He was dressed in a sharp black suit, with a black shirt open at the neck and a starkly white tie hanging loosely against his broad chest. He'd slicked his long fringe back with some kind of wax and it sat neatly against his head, apart from a couple of rogue strands which fell across his forehead, for once allowing his amazing bright blue eyes and strong jaw the exposure they deserved.

Flora's heartbeat thumped loudly in her ears as she stood staring at him, marvelling at how very different he looked. And how very different she suddenly felt.

But this was just Alex, she reminded herself sternly. Amy's scruffy, totally unsuitable brother. Who she was just friends with.

Just friends.

Realising that her mouth had become inexplicably dry, she swallowed hard and dragged her gaze away from Alex, making her way over to the bar to get herself a drink.

She'd just been served a large glass of white wine when she felt someone approaching from her right. Turning to look, she saw Alex making his way towards her, his usual confident swagger very much in evidence.

'Hey, you came,' he said as he drew close, giving her one of his stunning wide smiles.

For some reason her mouth didn't seem to want to do as it was told, so she just stood there grinning at him like a complete fool.

'You okay?' he asked, looking bemused.

Giving herself a mental shake she nodded, then cleared her dry throat. 'Yes, great. You look fantastic. Very dapper. Are you nervous? You must be. It's a big old place to fill. Not that I'm sure you won't fill it—' She finally managed to curb her babbling and gave him an apologetic smile. 'Sorry, I guess I'm a bit nervous for you.' The weird squeaky laugh that came out after that statement made her cheeks flush hot with embarrassment.

He just grinned at her, his eyes twinkling. 'Well, it's kind of you to take my nerves on for me, but I've got it covered.' She was sure she caught a momentary flash of trepidation in his eyes.

'Are you okay?' she asked, reaching out to rub his arm in a friendly gesture of solidarity, feeling a shock of concern at how tense his muscles were beneath his suit.

'Yeah, I'll be fine once we get started.'

In her peripheral vision Flora became aware of a man, also dressed in a sharp suit, walking towards Alex with stern intent written across his face. She gestured in his direction to draw Alex's attention to him. 'I think someone might need you.'

The man came to a stop next to them and she saw Alex give him a somewhat reluctant nod of acknowledgement.

'Alex, we need you backstage,' the man stated in a curt voice.

'Yeah, okay, I'll be there in a minute.'

His bandmate sighed. 'No, now, man. We don't have much time before this place is jammed.'

Alex's jaw flexed as he appeared to clamp it together hard. 'Yeah, I know that, Zane,' he said with ironic slowness, 'but I'm talking here. I'll be there in a minute.' He emphasised the repeated sentence with such force that Flora wondered what the problem was between them. Because there clearly was one.

Before the other man could respond there was

a flurry of sparkles beside them and a woman appeared at his side.

'Hey, guys. Everything okay here?' she cooed in a beautiful gravelly voice.

Flora turned her full focus to the woman and her eyes involuntarily widened. She was dressed in an ornately decorated flapper-style dress, which shimmered under the lights as she stood there gazing at them all with catlike yellow eyes. She was beautiful. Utterly stunning, with honey-coloured skin, full red-stained lips and glossy jet-black hair that had been styled into soft waves pinned away from her face, like they used to wear it in the nineteen-thirties.

'Yeah, we're fine,' Alex muttered with a scowl, only shooting the woman the most perfunctory of glances.

'And who's this?' she asked, giving Flora a curious smile.

'This is Flora,' Alex said, but from the sound of his voice he really didn't want to extend the introduction any further than that.

Was she really that embarrassing to be around?

The thought made a prickly shiver rush across her skin. Perhaps he was only being chivalrous when he'd said that she didn't need to wear make-up to look good.

Gritting her teeth, Flora flashed him a covert frown before turning back to the woman. 'Nice to meet you. I'm guessing you're part of the band too?'

'Yeah, I'm on vocals,' the woman said, extending a hand, which Flora shook, trying not to crush it as she felt how limp it was. Flora had never been one to hold back on a handshake, but this woman obviously didn't set the same store by them.

'So are you a friend of Alex's?' the woman asked with a strange inflection to her voice that made Flora think there was an undercurrent she wasn't a party to. Had they all been arguing before she got here? Or was there some sort of tension between this woman and Alex? The thought made her stomach sink in a peculiar way. Not that it wouldn't be great for Alex if he found someone new to fall in love with. Especially if she was musical too.

Her guess was thwarted though when the woman slid her arm around the other bandmate that Alex had spoken to so curtly and pressed herself against his side, smiling up at him in what was clearly a possessive and adoring manner.

Ah, so these two were a couple then.

So why had she been looking at Flora in such a strange way? It had actually felt a little unfriendly, if she was being honest. Was she worried Flora was going to break Alex's heart like his ex-girlfriend had?

When Flora turned back to glance at Alex she was surprised to see that he was deliberately avoiding looking at the overtly affectionate couple next to him. In fact he looked incredibly uncomfortable, as if he'd rather be anywhere but there.

Then it hit her, so hard it made her suck in a sharp breath, which she rushed to cover with a small coughing fit.

This was the woman who had broken Alex's heart.

And, to make things a million times worse, she was the lead singer of his band.

CHAPTER FIVE

ALEX HAD REALLY hoped to avoid a situation where Flora and Tia would come face-to-face, hence his reluctance to get Flora a ticket for the gig tonight in the first place. But the fates, it seemed, had had a very different idea.

He realised his mistake now, of course. He should have anticipated that Flora would turn up early and suggest she not come until the gig was just about to start, but in his state of comfortable equanimity after they'd been swimming last week it hadn't occurred to him.

Looking out over the large crowd while there was a short pause between songs and Tia did her usual cooing and joking around with the audience—something he used to love listening to but now made him want to chew his own hands off—he spotted Flora sitting at one of the tables in the middle of the room. A wine glass in hand, she watched Tia's performance with a quizzical frown pinching her brow. She had to have guessed who Tia was by now, he realised as the drummer started up the beat for the next song and he readied himself to play, but would she be bold enough to bring it up with him later?

Who was he kidding? Of course she would.

This was Flora we were talking about.

His cue came then and he lost himself in the music again, feeling for the first time in a while that he was getting his groove back. Despite his worry that his musical ability had completely deserted him recently, he was pleased with the way he was playing tonight. Every now and again he'd glance over to where Flora sat and see her smiling in what seemed to be mesmerised awe and it would give him a little boost that would carry him through to the next song.

Ironically, it turned out it was pretty great having her here to support him.

After they'd played their last song and Tia had bowed them off the stage, he rushed to say good-

bye to the other members of the band, waving
away their suggestion of a drink so he could go
find Flora. He was going to suggest that they
hightail it out of there and grab something to eat
somewhere a bit quieter in the hope she and Tia
wouldn't end up in the same vicinity as each other
again. He'd noticed the strange tension coming
off his ex-girlfriend in waves earlier and he didn't
want to expose Flora to any more of it.

Except Flora wasn't in the seat she'd been sitting in throughout the whole performance. Perhaps she was in the bathroom. He lingered there,
tapping his fingers against his leg impatiently as
he waited for her to reappear.

One of the audience members came up to him
as he waited, congratulating him on a great set,
and he fell into a conversation with him, his attention still half-focused on the corridor leading to the bathrooms. As soon as the guy moved
on to get a drink at the bar, someone else came
over, then someone else. He found himself field-
ing congratulations left, right and centre, which
gave him another lift he'd not expected from to-

night. He was just finishing up a conversation with a fan who turned up at all the band's gigs, and who told him she thought he'd played his best ever set tonight, when he spotted Flora walking towards him.

Politely excusing himself, he walked over to meet her. 'Hey, there you are,' he said, letting out a grunt of surprise as she walked into his arms and grabbed him round the waist, giving him a tight squeeze. When she pulled away his stomach lurched as he saw there were tears in her eyes.

'Oh, my goodness, Alex, you totally blew me away! You were amazing! I had no idea.' She looked a little sheepish now, as if admitting that she'd been anticipating a boring evening only to be utterly confounded by actually enjoying herself.

He grinned, pleasure pooling in his belly and heating his skin. 'Thanks for "giving jazz a chance",' he teased, smiling as he noted a flush rising to her face.

'We should get out of here,' he said, gesturing

towards the door where a large crowd of people were now exiting the venue.

'Really?' she said. 'Don't you want to stick around and have a celebratory drink with your bandmates?'

'What a great idea,' came a voice from behind him and he turned to see Pete, the band's trumpeter, with a tray of drinks in his hand. 'Let's grab this table while it's free,' he said, nodding to the one they were standing next to. He put the tray down on it, making the glasses rattle as they bounced against each other.

'I was going to take Flora out for some food,' he began to protest, but Pete waved away his excuse, picking up a pint of beer and thrusting it towards him. 'Don't be an idiot. You have to stay and have at least one drink with the band. We were stupendous tonight!' Alex caught the meaningful look in his friend's gaze and gave him a tight smile. Pete was well versed in the whole Tia debacle and clearly thought that running off now would be akin to letting her win.

'And here's one for your gorgeous lady,' Pete

said with emphasis, giving Flora a wink and passing her a large glass of wine, which she accepted with a smile of startled surprise.

'Oh, thank you! Well, I guess we should stay just for this one,' she said, looking at Alex for confirmation.

Obviously they couldn't leave now, not without it seeming really rude—or cowardly—so he raised his eyebrows and said, 'Yeah, sure. We can move on after this one.'

They all sat around the table and just as Pete started to ask Flora whether she lived in Bath, Zane and Tia came over to join them, taking the two seats next to her.

Alex tensed as he forced himself to look over at Tia, only to find her staring at Flora with a strange speculative look on her face. There was something a little hostile about it, not that she was being overt in any way, but he knew her too well not to pick up on things like that.

Perhaps she wasn't too happy with Flora crashing the band's celebratory drinks. Not that she had any right to complain about him bringing someone else. She'd been the one to call a halt to their relationship, after all.

'So, Flora, how did you and Alex meet?' Tia asked suddenly, leaning towards Flora a little and giving her that concentrated smile that he knew meant she was on the warpath about something.

Flora, to her credit, didn't even blink. Instead she sat perfectly still in her chair and fixed Tia with a cool, formidable sort of stare. 'Alex's twin sister was my best friend.'

So she'd definitely figured out who Tia was then.

There was an uncomfortable beat of silence during which the two women looked intently at each other, as if willing the other to look away first.

'Hey, Alex, what are your plans for Christmas?' Pete asked loudly, breaking into the strained atmosphere. Out of the corner of his eye he saw Flora turn away from glaring at Tia to look directly at him.

Heat began to creep up his neck as he remembered he'd told her he was spending Christmas

Day with the band, which in retrospect had been a little foolish, especially now he was about to be caught out in his lie. He hated to think how Flora would react when she realised he'd deliberately misled her. Especially when she was being such a loyal friend to him right now.

'Er...' he began, racking his brain for an answer vague enough to get him out of trouble.

Luckily the drummer, Des, shouted over him, 'Hey, Zane, I meant to ask, are you and Tia off to London on Christmas Eve or Christmas Day? 'Cos I'll hitch a lift with you if it's Christmas Day. I've promised my dad I'll go over there for lunch now.'

'Sorry, man, we're going on Christmas Eve,' Zane answered, glancing at Tia for her agreement.

'What *are* you doing for Christmas, Alex?' Tia asked, completely ignoring her boyfriend. 'I hope you're not spending it all on your own.' She was eyeing him now in a way that made him think she suspected he'd dug himself into a hole and was intent on exposing him for it. He wasn't sure why she thought she had the right to be so prickly with him, but he sure as hell could do without it right now.

He felt Flora shift in her seat next to him and he glanced round at her in panic, praying she wasn't going to have a go at him for fibbing to her and expose his pathetically lonely Christmas to the rest of the band.

'Actually, he's coming up to Derbyshire with me,' she said loudly, looking him right in the eye and giving him a slow wink that no one else could see. She turned back to Tia. 'I'm introducing him to my parents.' Looking back at Alex, she purred, 'They haven't had a chance to meet you yet, have they, honey?' The term of endearment was clearly proprietorial.

Tia's mouth fell open for a second before she caught herself and snapped it shut, forcing it into an artificial-looking smile.

'Wow, that's quick,' she said with a slight wobble in her voice. 'We had no idea he was even seeing anyone.' She ostentatiously slung her arm around Zane's shoulders. 'Did we?' She gave him a swift kiss before looking back their way again.

Flora gave a nonchalant shrug. 'Yes, well, it's been a bit of a whirlwind romance, to be honest. But we both knew it was right between us straight away, didn't we, gorgeous?' She turned to look at him now, giving him a wry but warm smile.

Before he could answer her, she looped her arm around his neck and pulled him towards her, pressing her mouth against his. He knew she was only doing it to show solidarity in the face of his awkward situation with Tia, but as she moved her mouth gently against his he had an intense sensory flashback to the last time she'd kissed him, remembering how she'd tasted the same way, sweet and sensual. For one fleeting second he wished this affection was actually real. His stomach did a weird swoop as he felt her lips part a little and the tip of her tongue sweep across his. And then, just as suddenly, she drew away from him and he was left staring into her sparkling green eyes in bewildered surprise.

'You're such a good kisser,' she cooed and his heart lurched with exhilaration until she gave him another covert wink and he knew for sure she was just laying it on thick for Tia's benefit.

There was a loud scraping noise as a chair was pushed back from the table. He tore his gaze away from Flora to see that Tia had stood up and was staring at him with such hurt in her eyes it took his breath away.

'I'm hungry,' she croaked, glancing away as soon as she noticed him looking at her. 'Let's go and get some food, Zane.'

Zane looked less than impressed with this sudden change in pace and tried to protest about being dragged away before he'd even finished his pint.

'I'll get you another one at the next place,' she snapped, spinning on her heel and walking stiffly away from the table, leaving Zane no option but to abandon his half-drunk pint and chase after her, calling a hurried goodbye to the rest of them.

When Alex glanced back at Flora she flashed

him a pseudo-innocent *What's her problem?* look, before breaking into a gleeful smile.

'I guess it's just us now then,' she quipped.

In that moment he felt something knit together inside him and he gave her a wide smile back, experiencing a sudden, forceful urge to take her away from here so they could be on their own. While he cared about his other bandmates and wanted to celebrate their success, he'd spent more than enough time with them recently.

'We should go and find somewhere to grab a bite to eat too,' he said to Flora, feeling a rush of relief when she nodded in agreement. He wouldn't put it past Tia to come storming back with a plan to disrupt the evening even further and he wanted to do everything in his power to avoid that.

As soon as they'd knocked back the dregs of their drinks and said a fond farewell to the rest of the group, they pulled on their coats and made for the venue's exit. Once outside, he turned to look at her with one incredulous eyebrow arched.

'What?' she asked, her eyes all wide and innocent.

'You kissed me again.' He shot her a look of mock consternation, mentally pushing away the small voice of hope that it hadn't all just been for show. She was being a friend, he reminded himself, carrying out Amy's last request of her. He felt pretty sure there hadn't been any more to it than that. 'You seem to be making a habit out of it,' he added with a smile.

Her cheeks looked a little flushed now. 'Er... yeah, sorry about that, but I wanted it to look authentic.'

'Well, thanks for stepping in and doing your duty as a friend.'

She gave him a slightly odd look, somewhere between a grin and a grimace. 'You're welcome.'

He gestured for them to start walking in the direction of the river, where there was an eatery with a roof terrace that had amazing views over the city.

'Tia seemed pretty annoyed by it,' Flora piped

up as they strolled side by side along the pavement, turning to flash him a mischievous grin.

He couldn't help but snort with mirth, his insides warming at the thought that they had a private joke between them now. It felt good. Now that he thought about it, he was surprised to find himself less concerned about what Tia was doing without him tonight than about how much fun Flora was having in his company. He'd been really made up with her effusive praise about his playing earlier and the euphoria seemed to have stayed with him.

'Where are we going anyway?' Flora asked as he motioned for her to take the next road on the right.

'There's a nice restaurant near the river. I thought we could try there. It's not the fanciest of joints, but I think it might fit even your exacting standards,' he joked.

He felt his stomach sink as he saw her frown, her eyes losing their smile.

'You must think I'm really stuck-up,' she said, letting out a loud sigh.

'Not at all.' He checked himself. 'Well, perhaps when I first met you. It was pretty obvious you weren't very comfortable in the pub I took you to, especially as I dragged you away from the Pump Room.'

'I just wanted to try it out. I'd heard loads of good things about it.'

He nodded, holding up his hands. 'I get that. And I'm sorry for pulling you out of there. As I'm sure you noticed, I wasn't in the best of moods that day.'

Her mouth twisted as if she was trying not to say something rude back about that.

'Hey, I tell you what. I'll take you there after Christmas to make up for it,' he offered. 'And I'll pay. You can't say fairer than that.'

He gestured for them to cross the road and led her past the sweeping grandeur of the Royal Crescent and on in the direction of the Assembly Rooms. 'It's not too much further up here,' he said.

'Good, because now that I've started thinking about food I'm suddenly starving,' she said with an emphasis that made him suspect that those glasses of wine on an empty stomach were beginning to have an effect.

He'd really rather avoid another incident like the last time they'd been drunk. Except for the kissing, perhaps.

Forcing that last rogue thought out of his head, he flipped her a grin. 'I'm sure they'll have something on the menu to suit even the most finicky of diners.'

He stepped to one side, laughing, as she slapped him playfully on the arm for his impudence.

'I'm not too proud to make you pay for that, you know,' she warned him. And he almost wished she would.

Three minutes later they reached their destination and hurried inside the boxy old brewery building, the rush of heat a welcome change from the biting cold.

'Let's go up to the terrace—they have great views up there,' he suggested, pointing to the wood and glass stairs that led up to the rooftop.

'Don't worry, they have heaters,' he assured her when she shot him an unsure look.

As luck would have it, there was a couple leaving a table right underneath one of the paraffin heaters as they walked onto the terrace. As they sat down, he caught Flora's look of pleasant surprise at the view laid out before them. The colourful lights of the city twinkled merrily against the heavy dark of the night sky and the river glided along gracefully in the distance.

'See, I don't just hang out in depressing pubs all the time,' he teased, catching her sheepish expression as the memory of their first meeting obviously came flooding back to her.

'Yes, it's really lovely up here,' she said, regaining her composure quickly and flinging him an apologetic grin.

How far they'd come since then, he mused.

They'd barely finished ordering their food when Flora crossed her arms and leaned back in her chair, fixing him with a stare that clearly meant business. 'So you're fine, are you? Playing in the same band as your ex-girlfriend and her new boyfriend.'

The highly sceptical look she gave him from under her lashes made him squirm in his seat. He rubbed his hand over his face, then held it up, palm forwards in capitulation. 'To be honest, no. It's really not fine. But you've heard her sing— she's incredibly talented and I think the band's going to do really well. I've worked so hard to get where I am so I'd be an idiot to throw it all in now.'

'You're really set on a musical career?'

'Yes. It's what I've always wanted to do. I tried a "real" job for a while and it made me miserable. I don't care about the money and fame, I just want to make music. It's the only thing that makes me truly happy.'

She nodded slowly, keeping her thoughtful gaze trained on him. 'Well, I have to say, you're damn good at it. Your playing really got inside me. It made me *feel* things.'

He couldn't help but grin at such a personal and intimate description. If he didn't know better, he'd say she was flirting with him. 'That's high praise indeed, coming from you.'

She shrugged. 'Yeah, well, I'm sorry for being so snippy before. I think I was just a bit nervous about meeting you, what with the upsetting circumstances and all.'

'You're forgiven. And I have to say, I'm delighted the dastardly cult of jazz has claimed a new member,' he said, lifting his hands and curling his fingers to look like some kind of evil, jazz-playing ghoul.

She laughed at this, throwing her head back in a way he'd never seen her do before. Perhaps she was finally beginning to properly relax around him. The thought made him inordinately happy.

Once their food arrived they were quiet for a while as they shovelled steak, chips and salad into their mouths, smiling and widening their eyes in pleasure by way of communication instead of talking.

'Okay, you're going to have to tell me what happened with Tia or it'll keep me awake at night wondering about it,' Flora said once they'd both finished eating. She wiped her fingers on her napkin and fixed him with a pleading stare.

He sighed, knowing there was no way to avoid telling her the whole sorry tale now. Dumping his cutlery on his empty plate, he leaned back in his chair and gave her his full attention, feeling his spirits sink at the thought of dredging it all up for her. 'To cut a long story short, we got together when we were living in London after meeting at a mutual friend's gig. We were the founding members of the band we play in now, which we pulled together by finding the other members through auditions. Apart from Zane. He was recommended by Pete, our trumpeter.' He tried not to frown as he remembered how uneasy he'd felt about Zane from the start, but Tia had convinced him to let the charming saxophonist stay.

'Those were some good times, when we first started playing together. It was clear right from the off that we really got each other's style and we were destined for the big time if we could just keep plugging away at it.' He took a long sip of his wine to soothe the roughness in his throat before continuing. 'Anyway, Tia decided that we needed to move out of London and focus our efforts somewhere where the scene wasn't over-saturated. I didn't really like the idea at first, but she talked me into it.' He shot her a grimace. 'She can be pretty persuasive when she wants to be.'

Flora just nodded, seemingly fascinated and intent on hearing the rest of the story.

'So we moved here and things were going great until Amy fell ill.' He took a shaky breath. 'I was suddenly spending a lot of time at the hospital with her and Tia started getting more and more annoyed about how little attention I was paying to the band—and to her.'

'What?' Flora said, shaking her head in baffled anger. 'Your sister was dying from cancer and she was throwing hissy fits about not getting as much attention as usual?'

He held up a hand. 'It wasn't exactly like that. To be fair to Tia, I completely failed to turn up for her birthday meal because I was so distracted, so she sat in the restaurant on her own for an hour before going home alone. And there were other things too. Things I'm not proud of.' He frowned, remembering with a thump of shame how he'd totally fallen apart when Amy had first told him that the cancer was terminal and he'd plummeted into a spiral of self-absorbed pity. 'As you mentioned the first day we met, I'm not exactly great at letting people in when I'm struggling to deal with things.'

She gave him a sad, understanding sort of smile, the effects of which he felt right down to his toes.

'I just kind of mentally checked out for a while. It was hard on her. I get that.'

'She didn't need to jump into bed with your bandmate though,' Flora said hotly.

Despite his humiliation, he still managed a smile at her show of loyalty.

'Yeah, having to watch the two of them together, day after day, it's—' He paused, wondering how he could put into words the soul-sucking agony he'd felt. 'It's been hard.'

'I bet.' Her expression was so empathic he wanted to lean across the table and kiss her for it.

He didn't though, because that wasn't what this relationship was about.

'You know,' she said slowly, leaning forward and spreading her long, elegant fingers out on the table in front of her, 'when I told Tia you were spending Christmas with me—' she locked her gaze with his and took an audible breath as if unsure how to phrase what she was about to say '—I would genuinely like that. I've made a commitment to see my parents for lunch, but we can duck out afterwards and hang out at a nearby pub and drink mulled wine next to a roaring fire.' She raised her eyebrows and added, 'If you fancy doing something like that.'

The mere idea of it gave his spirits such a lift he felt a bit dizzy from the rush of blood it sent to his head. He'd actually begun to dread spending the whole day alone now so her offer was most welcome. 'Won't your parents mind you leaving right after lunch?'

She broke eye contact with him to look down at her hands, which were busily realigning the salt and pepper shakers. 'They'll understand, I'm sure.'

But he wasn't sure that she really *was* sure.

'Look, I appreciate the offer but I don't want to interfere with your family's plans.'

There was a beat of silence before she met his gaze again. 'I'm sure my mum would love it if you came for lunch too.'

'Really?' he asked, still not entirely convinced.

Flicking back her hair, she gave him a firm nod. 'Yes. I'm positive. I'll give them a call to check tomorrow, but I'm ninety-nine per cent sure it'll be okay.'

Sitting back in his chair, he gave her a smile that rose from deep down in his belly. 'That would be great, Flora, thanks. It'll be interesting to see where you hail from.'

Was it his imagination or did she just hide a grimace?

'Did you say they're in Derbyshire?' he asked.

'Yes, just north of Bakewell, in the middle of the Peak District,' she said, her brow furrowed as if the thought of it gave her pain.

'Okay, well, since you're providing the entertainment, I'll drive,' he said.

'Great.' She nodded slowly. 'I was planning on travelling up on Christmas Eve to arrive late in the evening.'

'Works for me,' he said, pushing aside the maddening little voice that whispered, *Maybe her mother will get the wrong idea and we'll end up sharing a room.*

He had a feeling that little voice was going to be the death of him.

CHAPTER SIX

ONE WEEK LATER, on Christmas Eve, Alex found himself ringing the doorbell to Flora's flat, ready to drive them both up to Derbyshire for Christmas at her parents' house, wondering how in the heck his life had taken such an unexpected turn.

Amy was probably looking down on him right now and laughing herself silly.

The door swung open to reveal Flora with a slightly panicked look on her face. 'Oh, you're here! I'm not quite ready yet.'

'You were expecting me to be late, weren't you?' he said, narrowing his eyes.

She gave a nonchalant shrug. 'Maybe.'

'Well, I'm glad I'm not entirely predictable,' he muttered, walking into the vestibule. He shucked off his coat and toed off his shoes, feeling a wall of heat hit him. 'Wow, it's roasting in here.'

'Yeah, I hate being cold,' she said, taking his coat from him and hanging it neatly on a peg on the wall next to a whole row of her own in every colour and style possible, or so it seemed.

'Why do you need so many coats?'

She looked at him in surprise. 'To go with all my different outfits. And for the different seasons. Don't you have more than one?'

'Nope,' he said, pointing at the one she'd just hung up. 'That's it.'

She just shook her head, a mystified expression on her face.

'Why don't you go and wait in the living room? I won't be long,' she said, disappearing into her bedroom.

'Okay.' He wandered through to her living room, giving the sofa an affable nod. 'Hello there, my old friend.'

Walking over to the mantelpiece, he picked up a framed photo of Flora dressed impeccably, of course, shaking hands with an older guy wearing an expensive-looking suit. They were standing in front of the logo for Bounce soft drinks, the company she worked for.

There was an expression of pride in her eyes which made something twist in his chest, and he experienced a sudden rush of affection for her. He might not particularly value her choice of career but he was intensely aware of how hard she must have worked and how focused she must be to get to a position like that.

She really was a very impressive woman.

'That was on my first day as Head of Marketing,' Flora said behind him. He started, dropping the photo frame on the floor.

'Sorry,' he said, picking it up and checking he hadn't damaged it. 'You made me jump coming up so quietly like that.'

'I didn't realise you hadn't heard me,' she said, but she was smiling.

'Are you ready to go?'

She nodded. 'Yup. All packed. I just need to check all the windows are closed. Back in a sec.'

While she bustled around the place, clicking on a light here and pulling a blind there, he leaned against the wall, letting his gaze travel around the room.

'Is this all your furniture?' he asked when she came back in and held up her hands in an *all done* gesture.

'No. I rented this place fully furnished. Why do you ask?'

'I thought it seemed a bit old-fashioned for your taste. It's nice and all, but I imagined you as more of a modernist.'

'So you're tuned in to my taste now, huh?' She shot him a grin. 'Perhaps we've been hanging around with each other too much.'

He bristled at that, her comment making him realise it was a bit strange that he felt he knew her so well already. 'I'm just observant,' he muttered in response, shrugging off his discomfort and pushing away from the wall. They'd not spent *that* much time together, he mused. Amy had talked about Flora a lot. That was probably why he felt as if he'd known Flora for longer than he had.

Then something else occurred to him. 'So if

you're renting furniture does that mean you're not staying in Bath long?'

'Uh…yeah. Once this product launch is live I'm going back to my position in New York.'

'Oh. Right.' He was surprised by how disappointed he was to hear this. He'd just assumed that she'd moved back to England for good and that she'd be around to meet up with every now and again. He'd grown to appreciate her company now and found he didn't like the idea of her leaving.

'Anyway, I'm ready when you are,' she said, a little more loudly than was necessary.

She really did like things running to schedule.

'Okay, then let's get going,' he said, grateful for a distraction from the strange sinking feeling in his chest.

The roads out of Bath were predictably busy and Flora sat back quietly, letting Alex concentrate on getting them out of the city and onto the motorway.

It would probably take them around four hours

to get up to Derbyshire at this rate and she felt a little shiver of concern at the thought of having to make conversation all the way there. Hopefully he'd be happy to listen to the radio for a bit of it. Car journeys always made her lethargic and she liked to just stare out of the window and think when she was travelling. She often came up with her best ideas when she allowed her mind to wander like that. Blue-sky thinking. Or in this case, ominous grey sky. It looked as though it might actually snow this year for Christmas.

'Mind if I put some music on?' Alex asked when they were finally speeding along in the middle lane of the M4.

'Sure, that would be great.'

'We'll go for the radio rather than one of my jazz playlists, shall we?' he said with a teasing note in his voice.

'You've turned me around on jazz now, so I'm happy to listen to whatever you've got,' she said in her most magnanimous voice. She felt a bit silly now, having been so quick to dismiss a whole genre she'd hardly heard anything of. Evidently it was time to expand her horizons.

'Okay then,' he said, flicking on the stereo. 'Can you go into the music app on my phone, choose the top playlist and send it to "car" when it asks you.' He gestured towards his smartphone, which was sitting in the well between their two seats.

'Sure.' She did as he'd asked, then sat back as the dulcet tones of Nina Simone began to play through the speakers. When that track finished and Billie Holiday started singing 'Summertime', Flora's attention perked up. 'Hey, I know this one. Didn't Janis Joplin sing it?'

'Yeah, she did. I prefer Billie's version though.'

'It's beautiful,' Flora agreed, the emotion of the song sweeping through her and making her skin tingle.

To her surprise, Alex started singing along with the song, his voice a deep, sexy rumble. She turned to stare at him, utterly transfixed as the delicious sound prickled along her skin and made her heart beat faster.

'Join in if you know the words,' he said, flipping her a smile.

The thought of him hearing her less than impressive voice made her hesitate. She'd been ridiculed enough in the past about how untuneful it was to be wary about airing it in front of anyone.

'I won't judge, I promise,' he reassured her, obviously sensing her hesitation. 'I think everyone should sing. It's good for the soul. I don't care if you're not in tune. Just let rip and enjoy it. That's what music should be about. We've become too focused on getting things exactly right these days rather than doing it just for the joy of it. Music should be about bringing people together, not about being pitch-perfect.'

That struck a chord with her and in the spirit of coming together at Christmas she decided to throw caution to the wind and give herself permission to just go for it. There was something incredibly freeing about it once she'd got over the first sting of embarrassment. She turned to grin at Alex as they sang their way through the next couple of songs, which she knew quite well from other artists having covered them, though she still cringed when she hit a wrong note.

Alex didn't say a thing though; in fact he didn't seem to mind at all.

A little while later the playlist came to an end and the silence in the car made her long for more music. It had been wonderfully uplifting, singing the songs with him, and she was sorry it was over. She wanted to say something about how much she'd loved listening to his beautiful voice, but she didn't want to sound like a fawning idiot.

'Let's have the radio on for a bit now. I'd like to catch the news. That okay with you?' Alex said, raising his eyebrows in question.

'Sure.'

He nodded and pressed the button on the stereo to turn on the radio.

It took the whole of the news bulletin before she felt as if she'd gotten her composure back under control. As a song about driving home for Christmas started playing on the radio, she was able to sound casually offhand saying, 'You know, you've got an amazing voice. You should write your own songs and sing them.'

'Actually, I already do.'

'Really?' She turned to look at him, intrigued.

Keeping his eyes trained on the road ahead, he nodded. 'Yeah, I've made a few demos but I've not had any interest yet. There's a producer I've made contact with who's interested in hearing the next songs I produce, but to be honest I've not been in the mood to write for a while, what with Amy and everything…' He petered out. 'And it's a tough business. Really tough, especially trying to strike out on your own. It's pretty demoralising to keep getting knock-backs.'

'I bet. Well, good luck with it. Don't give up, okay? The people who make it are usually the ones who work really hard for years and keep getting back up after a rejection. Very few people are actually "overnight successes", but I guess you already know that.'

'Yeah, I get that.' He sighed and rubbed a hand over his brow. 'It'd be great to be able to run my own show. I love playing in the band—at least

I do when my ex-girlfriend's not fronting it—'
he shot her an ironic grin '—but the real satisfaction comes from writing and performing my
own songs.'

'That makes sense,' she said, warming to the
theme. 'It's important to maintain as much control over your brand as possible, which isn't an
easy task these days, because everyone wants a
piece of you when you're successful.'

'Has that been your experience?' he asked.

She snorted. 'It's a bit different for me. Marketing isn't the most sexy of professions.'

'But it's impressive how fast you've risen up
the ranks.' There was genuine warmth in that
statement and she gave him a smile of gratitude
for the recognition. It meant much more coming
from him than from anybody else because it had
been so hard-won.

'I don't know how you can work in a place
like that day after day though,' he said suddenly,
frowning hard at the road ahead. 'I think it'd
probably kill me. The years I spent after univer-

sity working for "the man" were the most miserable of my life.'

'Yeah, well, there are great prospects for career development at my company,' she said, feeling her shoulders stiffen at how forced that had sounded.

'Is your boss still giving you a hard time?' he asked after a pause.

She shot him a startled look, anxiety rising like a heatwave up her neck. 'Why do you ask that?'

'The first time we met you mentioned that he wasn't letting you do your job properly.'

It came back to her now. She *had* told him that in her drunken stupor. Damn it.

'It's fine. I can handle it. I'll win him over eventually.' She wished she felt as assured as she sounded. Her sister might have got the looks and musical ability, but Flora had always been damn good at her job—that was her talent. Which was why this particular challenge to her self-confidence was so unsettling.

'I'm sure you will,' he said and the affection

in his voice made her insides do a funny little dance of joy.

'Thanks for the vote of confidence,' she said.

'You're welcome.'

When she glanced at him he turned to meet her gaze and gave her such a warm smile she thought she might combust on the spot.

What was going on here? It seemed as though he was making a concerted effort to be nice to her now, but was she reading too much into it? Was it just because he was grateful that she'd invited him to spend Christmas with her?

Or was he beginning to actually *like* her?

'Hey, perhaps you could play some of your songs for me some time?' she said, indulging an urge to maintain this new level of connection between them.

He shrugged, seeming pleased by her interest. 'Sure, if you like.'

She did like. She did like a lot.

'Great.'

They sat in companionable silence for a while after that, listening to the radio, passing comment every now and again on a song or a news article. An hour away from their destination, Flora realised with a jolt of surprise that she hadn't felt this relaxed for a very long time. It was actually really nice to have someone else take the wheel while she sat in enforced stillness for once.

It was so pleasant she eventually dozed off, her dreams skating between memories from her life back in the States and the last few weeks she'd spent here in England. Then her dreams drifted to Christmases past, in particular the Boxing Day three years ago when she'd come downstairs in the morning and found her sister with an odd look on her face. Violet had laughed it off as a hangover from the heavy drinking the night before—the drinking that had sent Flora to bed early, leaving her sister and Flora's fiancé, Evan, alone with each other.

She'd known right then, deep down, what had happened. She just hadn't wanted to believe it.

Waking up with a jolt, she turned to look at Alex, who was frowning at the road in front of him as he navigated the windy A road towards her parents' house. The feeling of dread that had been sitting heavily in her stomach for the last few days began to crawl up her chest and into her throat. She knew she should warn Alex about the sort of atmosphere he was going to walk into and reassure him that they wouldn't have to stay for long.

Sitting up straight and taking a fortifying breath, she turned to look at his profile, giving him a tight smile when he glanced over at her.

'I should probably mention that my sister and her husband will be there as well tomorrow,' she said, hearing a shake in her voice. She crossed her arms over her chest, feeling hot and uncomfortable about what she was about to tell him.

'Great, it'll be nice to meet them too,' Alex said breezily.

She cleared her throat. 'Did Amy tell you the story about me and my sister, Violet?'

He glanced over and frowned, obviously picking up on her discomfort now. 'No.'

'Okay, well, I should warn you that there might be a slightly strained atmosphere between us.'

'Really? Why's that?'

'Because her husband, Evan, is my ex-fiancé.' She let that hang there for a second before continuing. 'We went out for eight months about three years ago and we got engaged two weeks before I brought him home for Christmas to introduce him to my family. After meeting my sister on Christmas Day, he dumped me on New Year's Eve so he could be with her instead. They got married just before I took the job in New York.'

'I see.' He nodded slowly, his expression neutral.

'I just thought I should mention it because Violet has a habit of flirting with any man I bring home—then going out with them when they decide they like her better.' She tried to sound offhand and jokey when she added the last part, but it fell totally flat.

She sighed, knowing there was no point in trying to make out she hadn't been heartbroken by it. 'It's been a bit of a repeating pattern, to be honest, going all the way back to our teenage years.'

'And you think she's going to hit on me?'

'I wouldn't put it past her, even with Evan there. She's always been a terrible flirt. And you're exactly her type. Musical and creative. And handsome.'

The heat in her face intensified as she realised she'd inadvertently admitted to Alex that he was *her* type too. At least he had been until Evan had smashed her heart to pieces and ground it into the dirt with the heel of his rock star–wannabe ankle boot.

'Take the next left,' she said, pointing to the entrance to her family's country pile, feeling nervous apprehension sink through her.

'We're here.'

They pulled up at the end of the sweeping driveway in front of what had to be a Grade II listed Georgian building, judging by the design of it. At a glance, Alex counted fourteen windows spread across three storeys. It was not so much a house as a small stately home.

'Wow, what a beautiful place,' he said to her.

Flora smiled back, her expression a little strained. 'Welcome to my not so humble abode.'

Clearly the thought of coming home for Christmas wasn't as joyful for her as it should have been.

Getting out of the car, he stretched out his back, feeling blessed relief at finally being able to get out of the cramped driving position he'd been sitting in for the last few hours. Then he went round to open the door for Flora. He wanted her to know that he was here to support her too, but didn't know how to put it into words without it sounding cheesy. He hoped his actions would speak for his intentions instead.

'Thanks,' she said with a smile, taking his proffered hand. He helped her stand up on the uneven gravel driveway in her heels.

'You're welcome,' he said, smiling back.

It made total sense now why she'd taken so much satisfaction in sticking it to Tia and why she'd invited him to spend Christmas with her: solidarity. She knew exactly how it felt to be passed over by someone you thought cared about you, then be forced to keep on seeing them whilst at your most vulnerable. In Flora's case the rejection and painful awkwardness seemed to have tainted her enjoyment of getting together with her family. He also suspected it had driven her to move all the way to the States to avoid it.

Grabbing the cases out of the car, he slammed the boot shut, then followed her as she walked stiffly over the gravel driveway towards the grand stone-pillared entrance to the house.

Her mother must have heard the car pull up because, before they had even reached the door, she'd swung it open and pulled Flora into her arms with a squeal of delight.

'Flora! It's so wonderful to see you. Merry Christmas!'

'This is Alex,' Flora said, disentangling herself from her mother's tight embrace and turning to gesture towards him.

He walked up to where they stood, noting

how much Flora looked like her tall, handsome mother, and held out his hand in greeting.

'Thanks so much for having me over for Christmas, Mrs Morgan, especially as it was so last-minute. I really appreciate it.'

To his surprise, she ignored his hand and pulled him into a tight hug too. 'Call me Diana. We don't stand on ceremony here.' She cocked her head in a sympathetic manner. 'Welcome to Winter Hall. It's wonderful to have you here celebrating Christmas with us, Alex. I was so sorry to hear about Amy passing away. It must be devastating to lose a twin sister, especially when she was so young.'

There was a heavy beat of silence in which Alex nodded in acknowledgement of her sympathy, his jaw clamping down hard as he pushed down the ever-present grief. 'It was. But Flora's been looking after me.'

He turned to smile at her and saw a pink flush rising on her cheeks.

'Er...well, we've been looking out for each other,' she muttered, not quite meeting his eye.

'Are Violet and Evan here yet?' Flora asked her mother, glancing around as if expecting them to spring out at her at any second.

'Not yet.' She paused, then fixed Flora with a pleading stare. 'Darling, please try and get on with your sister while you're here,' her mother said, her expression morphing into an anxious frown. 'She's not been herself recently. I think she and Evan might be having some problems, so she's going to need our support.'

'Like the way she supported me by whisking my fiancé away from under my nose, you mean?' Flora said, her words heavy with irony.

Her mother sighed. 'Oh, Flora, please tell me you're not still holding a grudge after all this time? You know she never meant to hurt you. Sometimes love works in funny ways.'

'Yes, hilarious,' Flora muttered, shrugging off her coat and hanging it on a peg by the door.

Alex felt a sting of anger on her behalf. Clearly Flora's mother had taken Violet's side in all this, which had to make Flora feel as if her sister was the favourite child.

There was the sound of wheels on the gravel outside and her mother turned away from them to hurry to the door and fling it open again.

Alex took the reprieve to hang up his own coat and draw Flora to one side. 'Are you okay?' he asked, searching her face for signs of distress.

She nodded. 'I'm fine, thanks. Just tired from the drive.' Her smile looked strained though.

'Is Evan not with you?' they heard her mother say as she ushered Flora's sister into the house.

'We had a row and he refused to come, but I don't want to talk about it right now,' a soft, husky voice replied.

As Violet walked into the wide stone-floored hallway, Alex felt his eyes involuntarily widen.

Flora's sister was stunning. She shone like the fairy light stars her mother had hung around the door frame, from the tips of her petite, stiletto-heeled boots to the ends of her sexily mussed-up baby-blonde hair.

Violet came to a sudden stop when she caught sight of him and he could have sworn she deliberately straightened her spine as she flashed him an inquisitive smile. 'Now here's someone I don't recognise. Who are you then?' she asked as she sashayed towards him, all thoughts of her missing husband apparently gone now.

Despite her beauty, there was something brittle and false about Violet that set Alex's nerves on edge. This was a woman who expected to be adored. He had a sudden urge to put his arm around Flora and protect her from the discomfort she had to be feeling right this minute.

'I'm Alex,' he said, not bothering to add his relationship to Flora. For some reason he didn't want to give her sister the satisfaction of knowing anything more about him.

'I'm Violet, Flora's sister,' Violet purred back. 'I know, we don't look much alike,' she added with a self-satisfied, conspiratorial smile, as if she found herself saying that on a regular basis.

An irritated shiver ran down Alex's spine.

Seemingly unaware of her narcissism, Violet's expression switched to one of pained distress, her large azure-blue eyes wide with sorrow. 'I'm afraid my husband, Evan, has decided he doesn't want to spend Christmas with me this year, so if you'll excuse me, I'm going to go up to bed.'

She gave her mother a brief hug. 'It's been a hell of a day and I'm exhausted.'

'Yes, of course, darling. Your room's all made up. We'll have a good chat about it in the morning.'

Violet nodded, her shoulders dramatically slumped, then turned to shoot him a quick seductive smile. 'It was lovely to meet you, Alex. I look forward to getting to know you better tomorrow.'

They all watched her walk away and mount the wide oak stairway before turning back to each other.

'Oh, dear,' her mother sighed, shaking her head.

Flora said nothing, just stood there stiffly.

He noticed that her usually sleek hair was mussed at the back where it had rubbed against the headrest for the last few hours and he had to forcibly stop himself from lifting a hand to smooth it down for her protectively.

'I think I might need to go to bed too,' she said

in a small, slightly strained voice, flashing him a look of apology.

'Fine by me,' he said. 'I'm pretty beat from the drive, so I'm happy to crash now.'

'Okay, well, Flora can show you where you're sleeping,' Diana said, giving them both a troubled smile. He guessed that this wasn't the joyful family reunion she'd been hoping for.

'Goodnight,' Alex said to her, nodding his thanks. Then, grabbing their bags, he turned to follow Flora up the staircase.

'Here you go, this is your room,' Flora said, gesturing towards the first door at the top of the stairs. 'I'm right next door,' she added.

Alex mentally gave the *little voice* the V-sign. There would be no sharing with Flora tonight then. Which was very much for the best. They would spend a lovely, warm and fuzzy Christmas together, then go back to their lives as even firmer friends.

Not allowing his overwrought mind to turn that thought into something inappropriately smutty, he handed over her bag and bade her a friendly goodnight. Then he let himself into his room with a shaking hand and flopped onto the bed, pulling the pillow over his head and letting out a long, low groan.

Tiredness. That was what this strange, nerve-filled tension was. He was *tired*, that was all.

CHAPTER SEVEN

THE NEXT MORNING Alex got up later than he'd intended after not sleeping well, despite the ultracomfortable bed he'd been given in the guest room. He stumbled down to the sunlit Breakfast Room to find Flora there drinking coffee and looking as though she'd been up for hours. Her hair appeared freshly blow-dried, her cashmere jumper and linen trousers were pristine and she was perfectly, and heavily, made-up. In stark comparison, he'd barely glanced in the mirror as he'd brushed his teeth and had only run his fingers quickly through his hair after showering before giving up on it.

'Good morning, or should I say afternoon?' Flora quipped good-humouredly, making a show of looking at her watch as he slumped into the chair opposite her.

'Merry Christmas,' he replied, looking around the well-appointed, high-ceilinged room that was empty of people except for them. 'Is your sister not up yet?'

She seemed to bristle at the question. 'No. She always sleeps in late.'

'And your parents?'

'They went to the morning church service.'

A young woman with a kitchen apron wrapped around her waist came in and gave him a friendly smile. 'What can I get you for breakfast? I can do eggs Benedict or a full English breakfast if you'd like.'

'This is Penny, my parents' housekeeper, who's very generously agreed to do the food today,' Flora said, giving the young woman a kind smile.

'It's actually my pleasure to be here,' Penny said. 'Anything to get away from the rows and tetchiness at home,' she added with a grimace. 'My parents don't get on at the best of times and Christmas Day seems to bring out the worst in them.'

'Well, in that case, I'd love eggs Benedict and

a cup of very strong coffee if you've got some on,' Alex said to her.

Penny gave him a nod of approval and left the room. He yawned behind his hand, hoping she wouldn't be too long with the coffee.

'Didn't you sleep well?' Flora asked, her brow wrinkling.

'Not really. It's a very comfy bed,' he added quickly when her face fell, 'but I'm still having trouble sleeping for more than a couple of hours on the trot.' He thought back to how he'd tossed and turned all night, his blood rushing with adrenaline and his mind whirring with tangled thoughts about Amy, his career, Tia and the band—and Flora.

'I have some relaxation music I can lend you— whale song and pan pipes, very soothing,' Flora suggested with a totally straight face.

He fought back a look of horror and forced himself to smile at her instead. 'Uh…no, I'm okay, thanks.'

She flashed him a wicked grin, making it clear she was teasing him.

He narrowed his eyes at her. 'Very funny.'

To his relief, Penny came back in then with a large mug of black coffee filled to the brim, which she placed in front of him.

'You are a truly magnificent woman,' he said to her, a little bemused to see a blush rise to her cheeks as she returned the smile, then scurried out of the room.

'You're such a charmer,' Flora said with an exaggerated eye-roll.

He just grinned back and picked up his mug, raising it to his lips. Those first few sips were like liquid joy.

'I thought we could go for a walk in a bit to get some air,' Flora said, looking out of the large picture window. 'It might snow later on, so we'd better not leave it too late.'

'Sure, whatever you like. I'm happy to go whenever.'

'Great.' She picked up the newspaper she'd been reading as Penny came back in with his eggs Benedict and they sat in companionable silence while he ate his breakfast. He made short work of it, his body crying out for energy after the rough night he'd had. When he finally put his cutlery down Flora smiled at him with amusement in her eyes.

'I thought you were going to scrape the pattern off the plate.'

'Hungry,' he growled in reply.

She just laughed and he thought how nice it was to see her looking more relaxed this morning.

'Let's take the papers through to the living room if you're finished,' Flora suggested, standing up when he gave her a nod of agreement.

The first thing he noticed when he walked into the elegant, tastefully decorated sitting room was a baby grand.

'Nice piano,' Alex said, walking over to it and tapping out a couple of notes, pleased to hear it was in tune. He missed playing when he was away from his instruments.

'Violet played it when she was younger.'

'I remember you saying. But you gave up.'

She scowled at this, apparently riled by his comment.

There was a flurry of movement in the doorway and Violet entered the room, wearing a pair of tight-fitting leather trousers and a bright red tank top, her sexily mussed up hair spilling over her slender shoulders.

Out of the corner of his eye he noticed Flora stiffen.

'I need another cup of coffee,' she said tightly. 'Want one, Alex?'

'Sure, I'll have another,' he said.

'Vi? Want a coffee?' Flora asked her sister, not looking at her as she made for the door.

'Yes, please, Floor, I'm going to be running mostly on caffeine today. I slept horrendously,' she grumbled, walking further into the room as Flora exited.

Alex left the piano and went to sit down on one of the Queen Anne sofas that stood on either side of the large marble fireplace.

'So, Alex, how did you and Flora meet?' Violet asked as she came and sat down right next to him, tucking her legs under her and leaning in towards him so their heads were only a couple of feet apart.

'Flora is my sister's—' he paused and took a breath '—*was* my sister Amy's best friend.'

Violet frowned. 'Oh, they're not friends any more? I thought they were really close?'

'Amy died from inflammatory breast cancer almost two months ago. It was a vicious strain that metastasised really quickly. There wasn't much they could do for her. The treatment they gave her didn't have much of an effect because the cancer was so fast-moving. It had already spread to her major organs.'

He was aware that his voice had become rougher as he had talked.

Violet looked shocked. 'Oh, my goodness, I hadn't heard. I'm so sorry.' She tipped her head sympathetically. 'Flora and I haven't spoken for a while. There's been a bit of tension between us since I married Evan.' She paused, her brow furrowing. 'They were engaged briefly before I got together with him.'

'So I heard,' he said coolly, noting how quickly

she'd turned the focus of the conversation back to her.

'I'm so pleased she's got you now though. It's great you're able to comfort each other at such a difficult time.' She gave him a kindly smile, obviously hoping to curry favour.

'We're just friends.' His voice sounded stiffer than he'd meant it to.

Her brows shot up. 'Really? I'm surprised. You two look so comfortable together. I thought you were a couple.'

He shrugged, feeling tension in his shoulders. 'We've been spending a lot of time together recently.'

There was a spark in Violet's eyes that made him uneasy. She put a hand on his leg and gazed right into his eyes, opening her mouth to say something just as Flora walked back into the room holding a tray laden with cups of coffee.

She had a pinched expression on her face as if something was giving her pain.

'Hey, great,' he said, springing off the sofa to relieve her of the tray, feeling a pull of guilt that she'd seen the weird scene between him and her sister and had probably misinterpreted it. Which wasn't surprising, considering the history of her sister flirting with her boyfriends. 'Thanks, Flora,' he said, making sure to give her a reassuring smile and hoping she'd know he was on her side here and that he hadn't been flirting with Violet.

There was more movement at the doorway as first her mother, then a man who he assumed must be her father, walked in bringing with them the scent of cold winter air from their trip to church.

'Aha, you're all up! Good. We can have a few games of charades before lunch,' Flora's mother said gleefully.

Both of her daughters rolled their eyes, but their mother wouldn't accept any grumbling protests. Flora's father walked over and introduced himself while the women argued about the rules, giving Alex a friendly smile and telling him to call him Francis.

They played a few games, with Flora, Alex and

Francis on one team and Violet and Diana on the other. It was a little strained at first, but after a while they all began to get into the spirit of it. There were even a few giggling moments when someone made a particularly suggestive motion.

Just as Alex uncovered the mystery behind a strange and rather uncomfortable-looking move Diana was doing with her head, Penny came into the room to let them know that their Christmas dinner was ready.

'We'd better go and take our seats,' Diana instructed them. She hustled Violet and Francis out before her, leaving Flora and Alex alone in the room.

'I'm so sorry,' Flora muttered, wrapping her arms around her body.

'About what?' Alex asked, not sure what she was talking about.

'About the strange atmosphere.'

'It's fine, Flora. I'm having a good time. I'm glad to be here.'

She sighed and rubbed a hand over her face, then picked a bit of fluff off her jumper and threw it towards the crackling fire. 'Okay...well, good.' She paused as if she was going to ask him something, then seemed to change her mind with a small shake of her head. 'I guess we'd better get in there,' she said instead, making it sound more like they were about to attend a state execution than enjoy Christmas dinner with her family.

They made their way into the dining room and took their seats. Flora was discomfited to find herself sitting directly opposite Violet, with Alex between them at the head of the table.

'I'd like to propose a toast,' Francis said, raising his wine glass and waiting till they all did the same. 'To our girls for being here to celebrate Christmas with us. And to our guest, Alex. May the next year be a better one for you all.'

'Cheers,' they all said quietly, each apparently thinking about the difficulties they'd faced throughout the year.

'Tuck in, everyone,' Diana said in an overly bright voice to cut through the suddenly sombre atmosphere, waving a hand at them before picking up her own knife and fork.

They were all quiet for a while as they ate the magnificent meal that Penny had prepared for them.

'It's so lovely to have everyone together again,' Diana said eventually, smiling around the table. 'Apart from missing Evan, of course,' she added.

Violet gave her mother a sad little nod of acknowledgment but didn't say anything. Flora was feeling so tense sitting across from her sister that her shoulders actually ached. It was always like this when she was in the same vicinity as Violet these days.

She took a deep steadying breath, grateful for the comforting heat of Alex's presence next to her, but wishing she'd cancelled on her parents and suggested they stay at a nice hotel instead now. Not that her mother would have stood for that. She'd been upset last year when Flora hadn't come back home for Christmas, citing her job in New York being too busy to allow her to get away.

As if reading her mind, her mother said, 'I know how expensive it is to fly over from the States, Flora, so it's wonderful you've been able to come this year.'

Her mum had no idea that she earned enough to fly home every month if she wanted, but she wasn't going to point that out right now. She already felt bad enough about avoiding coming here to see them.

'Yeah, it's nice to be here,' she said and smiled, blotting out the small voice whispering *Liar* in her ear.

Penny came in then and saw that they'd all just about finished. 'We have Christmas pudding or trifle for dessert if anyone can manage it,' she announced as Alex put his knife and fork down on his empty plate.

'Yes, please. I'd love both of those, in the same bowl is fine,' he said, leaning back in his chair, patting his belly and blowing out his cheeks in a over-the-top satisfied manner, making Flora smile for the first time since they'd sat down.

After they'd finished dessert they retired to

a toasty-warm living room and brought out the presents they had for each other.

Flora found she was actually looking forward to seeing her parents open the gifts she'd bought for them this year.

'Here you go. Happy Christmas,' she said, passing Violet a gift bag with a cashmere jumper and some expensive bath smellies in it. Then she handed a bulging gift bag over to her mother so she could divide her parents' presents up between them.

'Oh, darling, you shouldn't have bought us so much. We don't need anything,' her mother admonished, tipping the presents out onto the floor and picking one up to examine it.

'It's fine. I wanted to treat you.'

Her parents spent the next few minutes carefully unwrapping all their gifts. They built themselves a small pile of all the designer clothes she'd bought hastily from her favourite Internet clothing outlet because she'd been too busy at work to go Christmas shopping, giving the odd 'hmm' or 'ah' as they held each item up briefly to glance at it before adding it to the mound.

'Thank you, darling,' her mother said eventually, giving Flora what felt like a very condescending smile.

'I thought you might appreciate some new clothes,' Flora said stiffly, the anticipated excitement of them being overjoyed with the things she'd picked out quickly draining away.

'We do,' her mother said, as if she'd just begged them to say something nice to her.

'Thanks, Floor,' Violet said, pulling on the jumper she'd been given, which of course looked like a million dollars on her.

'You're welcome. Thanks for the make-up,' she said, gesturing to the little boxes of anti-ageing cream, eye gel and concealer her sister apparently thought she needed.

'Here you go. This is from us,' her father grunted, handing over the customary Christmas cheques he always gave his daughters. Their mother gave them each a small pile of wrapped presents.

Flora tore the wrapping off a framed painting by an artist she'd loved since she was a teenager and squealed with delight, giving both her parents a hug of thanks. Then she picked up a small flat package, pulling off the paper to look down at the book she'd been given: *Living the Good Life: How to grow your own food.*

'I thought it might come in handy,' her mother said.

'Er… Mum, I don't even have a garden,' she said with a bemused grin.

'But you might one day soon, once you get fed up with living in New York and move back here to England.' Her mother gave her a hopeful look.

Pushing a feeling of guilt quickly aside, she forced herself to smile at her parents. 'Thanks very much. I'm sure it's got some great ideas in it.'

'You're most welcome, my darling. Make sure you spend the money frivolously too. That's what it's for.'

'And this is for you, Alex,' her father said, turning to him and handing over a squashy parcel.

'Sorry it's only small, but we didn't get much warning about you coming,' he added, giving Flora an admonishing glance.

'Oh, wow. Thank you. I really wasn't expecting anything. That's really kind of you,' Alex said, pulling a gorgeous forest-green jumper out of its wrapping paper. He beamed at both of her parents, genuinely pleased with it and grateful for their generosity, then pulled it over his head.

'It suits you,' her mother declared, clearly delighted.

'Yeah, you look great in it,' Flora said, intensely aware of the undisguised admiration in her voice.

There was a short silence where she caught her parents smiling at each other covertly and she felt her cheeks heat with embarrassment.

'And this is just a very small present, to say thanks for having me today,' Alex said, breaking into the awkward silence and producing a wrapped gift.

'Ooh, how lovely of you!' her mum exclaimed, taking it from his proffered hand. She carefully tore off the paper to reveal a recordable CD case.

'It's a collection of some of the best jazz and blues tracks ever written,' he explained. 'Some are a little obscure, but hopefully you'll come to love them.'

'Oh, Alex, what a wonderful thought! We love listening to music. How very kind of you,' her mother gushed as her father reached across and gave him a pat on the back.

Flora stared at them all, wondering whether she'd somehow moved unwittingly into the *Twilight Zone*.

'We can all listen to that later on, whilst we're eating our supper,' her mother said, going over to the stereo system they had hidden in a mahogany sideboard and laying the CD reverentially on top of it.

'We weren't planning on staying for supper. We should probably hit the road before there's a mad rush,' Flora said quickly.

Her mother's face fell. 'Oh. Really? Can't you stay tonight? I was hoping we could keep you here a little longer.'

Flora stiffened, steeling herself against the

wave of guilt she felt about making an excuse to hurry out of there, but before she could open her mouth she heard Alex say, 'That would be great, Diana.' He turned to look at her. 'We can stay again tonight, can't we, Flora? Perhaps I could play the piano after we get back from our walk and we can all have a sing-song?'

'What a wonderful idea!' Her mother sounded utterly delighted by the suggestion.

Flora covertly raised her eyebrows in an *Are you kidding?* look at him, but he held fast, keeping his expression neutral but firm.

She let out a long sigh, knowing when she was beaten. 'Okay, yeah, sure. That would be fun,' she said flatly.

'Great! That's settled then,' her mum said, sounding happier than she'd heard her in a long time. Even her usually taciturn dad was nodding and smiling with pleasure.

Flora smiled stiffly, then slapped her hands lightly on her knees. 'Okay, well, we should probably go out for that walk before the heavens open. You still fancy it, Alex?'

Gratitude poured through her when he nodded and smiled. 'Sure.'

'Great. Let's go now then.' She got up and smoothed down her trousers, relieved at the thought of a little respite from her sister's perturbing presence.

'What's the matter?' Alex asked Flora as soon as they'd closed the front door behind them. They were both wearing warm coats, hats, gloves and the walking boots she'd suggested they pack in anticipation of exploring the fifteen acres of land surrounding Winter Hall.

She shrugged her shoulders and waved her hands about, as if unable to form the words.

'What, Flora?'

'It's just—'

'Yes?'

'I thought you'd want to get out of here, that's all,' she said, looking utterly exasperated.

'Nah, I'm fine. And I think your parents are really pleased you're staying on a bit longer. It was obvious they were hoping you would. They clearly miss you.' He gestured for them to start walking and they set off towards a clump of trees in the distance.

'Hmm,' was all she said to that, folding her arms and glaring up at the sky, which looked ominous and brooding.

The moody light made him suspect it was about to snow. Just as he thought this, he saw a snowflake drift down and land in Flora's hair.

'Flora?'

She looked at him with a frown. 'Yes.'

'You haven't told them that you're living in Bath at the moment, have you?'

Embarrassment flickered across her face. 'No.'

He sighed and shook his head. 'Coming from someone who has no family left, I recommend trying to bridge that gap. I think Amy would have wanted that for you. You shouldn't be alienated from the people who clearly love you.'

Flora sighed, pushing a strand of hair out of her eyes. 'Yeah, I know that. She was always encouraging me to see more of them.' She took a breath. 'I will tell them I'm over here for a bit.

It's just that I'm not going to be here for much longer and I didn't want them to get all excited about me being back only to have me leave almost immediately again.'

His chest gave a weird throb at that, but he ignored it and just nodded sagely at her.

They were quiet for a moment as they strolled along side by side, with only the sound of distant bird chatter breaking the silence.

'Is something else bothering you?' he asked tentatively. He'd felt her tension when they were exchanging gifts and he was pretty sure something had really upset her. 'Something about the presents?'

'You gave my parents a music playlist!' she blurted, turning to glare at him now.

'Ye-e-s,' he said slowly, baffled by why that should incense her.

'I gave them a big pile of designer clothes and they were more impressed with a CD you knocked up in ten minutes.'

He couldn't help but laugh. 'It's not about how much money you spend on a present, you know.'

But his amusement only lasted briefly, draining away when he saw her face fall and hurt spark in her eyes.

'Apparently the latest fashions in luxury fabrics stand no chance against a few old songs thrown together right before getting into the car.'

'Actually it was the night before, but who cares,' he replied, taking a quick step backwards when he saw the look of mock-murderous intent this quip provoked.

'You're such a kiss-ass,' she grumbled, shooting him a wry grin to show she was only kidding around.

He grinned back. 'I'm just trying to get into their good books. I'm very grateful for them agreeing to let me come here at the last minute.'

'Well, I think we can safely say you've made it in there. My mum's going to start dropping hints about wanting grandchildren soon, thanks to you.'

'You don't want kids?' he asked.

'Sure. One day. I guess I'll think about it once

I've got a steady partner. I've been too busy with my career to give it much thought.'

'But you'd consider it?'

'Yeah. If I had a partner who was willing to share the childcare and housekeeping. I wouldn't want to give up work full-time to look after kids. It just wouldn't be for me.'

'Fair enough,' he said.

There was a tense silence when they just looked at each other. The snow was coming thick and fast now, settling on the ground under their feet so it made a quiet crunching sound as they walked over it in their boots.

'We should probably head back before we get snowed under,' she said, clapping her hands together to try and warm them up.

'Yeah, sure,' he said, a little disappointed to be going back now. He was really enjoying being with her out in the winter wonderland. They turned towards the house, which was a vision of cosy comfort, its windows glowing with soft, welcoming light.

'You know, they probably only reacted like that

about the presents you gave them because they'd rather have something a bit more personal from you,' he said, feeling a strong urge to change the subject back to the one that she clearly needed to talk about.

She gave him a confused and slightly irritated frown. 'What do you mean?'

Holding up his hands, he leaned away from her in an exaggerated manner. 'Hey, don't shoot the messenger; I'm just making an observation. Your parents have surrounded themselves with things that mean something to them. There are photos of you and your sister everywhere and what looks like every piece of artwork you've ever produced covering all the surfaces in the dining room.'

She shot him a pained smile at this. 'Yeah, there are some real beauties on public display.'

'What I mean is, they're probably not overly concerned with having a big pile of expensive *stuff*. They like things that speak to them. Things that make them feel.'

He saw her shoulders slump a little.

'Yeah, you're probably right.' She took a

shaky-sounding breath, as if steeling herself to say something difficult. 'I guess I've always felt this desperate need to please that stems from my childhood. Violet was very clearly their favourite and I figured out that if I wanted to impress them I had to work really hard and get exceptional grades. Then, after uni, a really good job. So that's what I did. I worked and worked and worked. I buy them impressive-looking presents to reiterate my success because I'm still trying to make them proud. Ugh!' She rubbed a hand over her eyes. 'It all sounds so pathetic when I say it out loud like that.'

'It's really not,' he reassured her. 'I understand why you'd act like that.'

Her expression looked pained. 'Perhaps my obsession with status has got a bit out of control now though.'

She came to a stop as they reached the front door to the house and turned her head to peek at him and gauge his reaction.

Twisting his mouth a little, he nodded at her. 'Yeah. It kind of seems that way.'

She let out a long-suffering sigh. 'I know I should be grateful for having parents that care about me. But my hang-ups about being second best to my sister are just so ingrained in my psyche now.'

He nodded slowly. 'Well, they certainly love you and they're delighted you came today. That's totally clear.'

'Thanks for saying that. It means a lot to hear it.'

There was something in her voice that made him look harder at her. She gazed back, her eyes filled with warmth, and his insides did an almighty flip, sending little thrills racing along his nerve endings.

She really was an incredibly attractive woman, as well as one of the kindest, smartest people he'd ever met.

And she *got* him.

The low winter light played over her refined features and for those few suspended seconds while she gazed at him he imagined what his life would be like with Flora permanently in it.

Her lips parted, as if she was about to say something else, and he leaned forwards, his own lips tingling and parting as the strongest urge to kiss her took hold of him. The look in her eyes flared, as if her pupils had darkened, and he dragged in a stuttered breath, his heart suddenly racing a mile a minute.

Then, most frustratingly, the door swung open to reveal the ever-distracting vision of her sister, dragging them both out of the intensity of the moment and back into the cold reality of the present.

'Hi, guys,' Violet said chirpily.

'Hi,' Flora answered with a strange wobble in her voice.

Alex cleared his throat, experiencing a sudden need to have a few moments on his own, to get his head round the disconcerting sensations racing around his body right now. 'I'm just going to nip up to my bedroom and change. I'm going to be too hot in all these layers,' he said, gesturing to the extra clothes he'd put on for the walk.

'Okay. I'll be in the living room,' Flora said,

not looking at him as she pulled off her boots and outdoor wear, then walked off in that direction, her shoulders stiff once again.

When he came back downstairs after taking a few deep breaths to calm his raging pulse, Violet was standing at the bottom of staircase, watching him as he descended.

'How was your walk?' she asked, giving him an inquisitive smile.

'Fresh,' he said carefully.

His initial attraction to Violet had definitely worn off now. He found her need to be adored and admired tedious. Now it just came across as a glossy but utterly superficial kind of allure, unlike Flora's subtle beauty that grew on you the more you got to know her.

'You've got snow in your hair,' she said, reaching up to brush it away with her fingers.

He took a small step back away from her, not wanting to give her any encouragement at all.

'Oh, look. We seem to be standing right under the mistletoe,' she said with a twinkle of mischief in her eyes.

He smiled thinly. 'Sorry, I only kiss very special people.'

'Like my sister,' she said, raising a suggestive eyebrow.

'I told you, Flora and I are just friends.'

'Uh-huh,' she said, sounding entirely unconvinced.

'I'm sorry I didn't get to meet your husband,' he said pointedly.

'Yes, me too.' Her face fell. 'Ugh! Why does life have to be so complicated? I'm sure Flora's told you all about what a hussy I am, stealing her boyfriends. But you have to understand what it was like for me spending my whole childhood in the shadow of someone so smart and superb at pretty much everything she did. Yes, maybe I got the looks, but she definitely got the brains. Sometimes Evan looks at me like I'm completely stupid and I know he's thinking he made a mistake choosing me over my brilliant sister.'

'That's not how she sees it,' Alex pointed out.

Violet let out a loud sigh. 'No, I know that.' She gave him a pleading look. 'I feel awful about hurting her, but I really, truly fell head over heels in love with Evan.' Her eyes filled with tears now. 'He's my entire world. I don't know what I'll do without him.'

Alex took pity on her. Clearly she was in a panic about her marriage ending and just needed someone to listen and maybe point her in the right direction. Strangely, it seemed that person was to be him.

'Look, why don't you give him a call and ask him to come over and talk? He's probably sitting alone at home feeling exactly the same way as you. Someone has to be the bigger person and break radio silence, otherwise it's just going to drag on and get harder and harder to communicate.'

'You think I should?' Her voice shook now.

'Yes. Better do it sooner than later, when he's already worked his way through half a bottle of Scotch.' He took a breath. 'My sister dying so young has really brought home to me that we have to grab our chances when we can. Why waste time not being with the person you love?'

She took a deliberate step backwards, grim determination flashing in her eyes. 'You're right. I'm not giving up on this marriage. I'm going to call him and tell him I love him and say that we need to work this out.'

'Good,' Alex said, smiling as he saw her square her shoulders and tip up her chin.

But, before turning to go, she leaned in close to him, looking him dead in the eye, and whispered, 'I don't believe for a second there's nothing between you and Flora. I saw the way you were looking at her when I opened the door, and how uptight she gets every time I get within touching distance of you. It's clear you're crazy about each other. So let me give you that advice right back. Don't wait too long and lose her, because my sister is an incredible person and you'd be a fool to let her slip through your fingers.'

And with that parting shot she strode away.

CHAPTER EIGHT

FLORA STEPPED BACK from the living room door, her heart racing and her hands shaking as the conversation she'd just overheard between Alex and her sister raced around her brain.

Alex had refused to kiss Violet.

Now that she thought about it, Vi was the only woman she'd not seen him flirt with, which was surprising coming from a man who flirted with everyone—well, everyone except for her, of course, but then their relationship was complicated. He'd even been charming with her mother when they'd first arrived—but not Vi, even though she'd made a couple of deliberate plays for him.

Alex had to be the only man she'd brought home who had resisted her sister's charms.

Her thoughts flew back to a few minutes ago

when she could have sworn he was about to kiss her, just before Violet had swung the door open and broken the intense moment that had passed between them. Her insides had leapt in confusion and she'd not known quite how to deal with the idea of it. She'd been relieved when Alex excused himself so she could have a moment to get her head together away from his befuddling presence.

And now this had happened and she had no idea what to think about it.

'Oh, Alex, you're back.' Her mother's voice rang out in the hallway. 'Perhaps you could play something on the piano now and we'll have that sing-song,' she suggested hopefully.

'Sure. I'd be happy to,' Flora heard Alex reply.

She quickly stepped back from the door and rushed to sit down on the sofa, her heart racing, not wanting to be found standing there eavesdropping.

Alex strolled in and sat down at the piano, turning to flash her a smile.

'You don't mind playing, do you?' she asked quietly before the others came in.

'Of course not. It'll be fun. We'll sing some Christmas songs—ones that everyone knows,' he added.

'Don't you need the sheet music?' she asked dubiously.

'Nope, it's all up here,' he said, tapping his head.

'Okay then.'

Alex began to play 'White Christmas' on the piano and she listened as music filled the room, feeling a sudden lift in her mood. It was funny, but music seemed to be having a much more intense effect on her since she'd met Alex.

Her mum came bustling in with a tray of tea and she helped herself to a mug, taking a quick sip to soothe her dry throat before putting it carefully onto the side table.

'Ooh, Alex, that sounds wonderful!' her mother cooed, going to stand next to him at the piano.

He turned to give her a smile and she beamed back at him.

'Thank you,' Alex said, still playing the tune, only a little more softly now so they could talk.

Her mother sighed. 'I wish Flora had learned to play the piano too when she was younger but because Violet was learning she steadfastly refused. Sibling rivalry, I don't know! They used to get on so well when they were little,' she added sadly.

'It was demoralising that she was so good at it when I could barely pick out a tune,' Flora pointed out.

Her mother frowned, her expression clouding with confusion. 'You would have been a great piano player, I'm sure, darling. You could always do anything you set your mind to.'

The affectionate look of pride she gave her now made Flora's chest contract, but before she could reply her dad strolled in and parked himself next to her on the sofa, slapping his hands loudly on his thighs.

'Right then. Are we going to have this sing-song now? I've warmed my voice up,' he said, rubbing his hands together. The next thing she knew he began to sing along with the tune that Alex was playing.

Taking this as a cue, Alex began to play more loudly and joined in with her dad's rather wonky rendition of 'White Christmas'.

After a beat her mum joined them and Flora had no option but to sing along too.

At the end they all smiled round at each other and her mother asked, 'Is Violet not joining us?'

'She said she needed some time out,' her father answered, exchanging a meaningful glance with her.

Flora wondered whether they knew about Alex's suggestion that Vi call Evan.

Before she could ask, Alex began playing 'Let it Snow! Let it Snow! Let it Snow!' and she couldn't help but join in. After that it was 'Hark! The Herald Angels Sing' followed by 'Rudolph the Red-Nosed Reindeer'.

At the end of that one, they all fell about laughing and Flora realised to her absolute astonishment that she was starting to have a really good time at home with her family. And Alex. He was the crux of it, of course.

They took a short break to drink whisky cream, or sweet sherry in her mother's case, and throw a couple more logs on the fire.

There was a loud knock on the door just as Flora and her mum were arguing about which song to sing next and they heard Violet shout, 'I'll get it. It'll be for me,' out in the hallway.

Flora saw her mother and father exchange looks of relief and, to her surprise, she found that she was actually pleased that there was a glimmer of hope for her sister and Evan. Being here with her family, and with Alex, had made her realise exactly what she'd been missing whilst away on her own in the States. She was determined to put the whole Evan debacle behind her now. It was definitely time to move on.

They heard the couple's voices recede as they went upstairs and slammed a bedroom door shut behind them. Then Alex launched back into a variety of carols and popular Christmas songs which they all demanded he play in turn. About an hour after he'd started playing again, Alex finally got up from the piano stool and came to sit next to her on the sofa.

Francis let out a loud yawn, then waved a hand in apology. 'All this singing has worn me out. I think I'm going to retire to bed and let you youngsters enjoy the rest of your evening,' he said.

Diana let out what seemed like a suspiciously fake yawn too. 'You know, I think I'll come with you, Francis.' Bustling over to the sofa, she leaned down to give Flora a tight hug.

'It's been so lovely having you here today. I hope you'll be able to make it back to see us again soon, my darling. You're always welcome here, you know that, right?'

Flora nodded against her mum's shoulder. 'I do. It's been lovely today.' She actually meant it for once.

'Alex,' her mother said, letting Flora go and enveloping him in a big hug next. 'It's been wonderful to have you here for Christmas. Thank you for looking after Flora for us,' she said, pulling back to look him directly in the eye. 'I've never seen her looking quite so relaxed,' she mock whispered. She winked, then flashed Flora a cheeky grin.

Flora dug her nails into her palms, but managed a wry smile in return.

'It's been lovely, Diana. Thanks again for having me,' Alex said, grinning, as she drew away from him.

'Well, goodnight, kids,' Francis said, backing out of the room with a wave. 'And Merry Christmas.'

'Merry Christmas,' Diana called too as she followed him out. 'Don't do anything I wouldn't do.' She paused. 'No, forget that! Do everything!' she said, clearly very tiddly now on sweet sherry.

And then they were alone again.

'Sorry about my mother, the Queen of Subtlety,' she said, rolling her eyes.

Alex just smiled. 'She's great. Both your parents are. I feel really welcome here.'

'Yeah, they're okay, I suppose,' she joked nervously as she suddenly became acutely aware of how close they were sitting in the otherwise empty room. She slapped her hands on her knees awkwardly. 'Well, that was fun. Thanks so much for all the music. I think my parents really enjoyed it.'

He turned his head to smile at her, his eyes dancing with amusement. 'You're welcome. I enjoyed it too. It's been a while since I've played just for fun. I'd forgotten how rewarding it can be.'

'Yes, I bet. That hadn't occurred to me,' Flora said thoughtfully. 'Well, it was wonderful. It gave me the tingles to listen to you.'

He arched an eyebrow. 'Ah, you're talking about *frisson*.'

'I'm sorry?'

'*Frisson*. It's a well-known phenomenon. Some people don't get it, but it sounds like you do, which is lucky for you.' He flipped her a smile. 'It's an emotional response to music. It starts as a rush of chills in the base of your spine, which then moves across your skin, making all your hairs stand on end. A bit like a skin orgasm.'

She swallowed hard. 'Er…yes. That's exactly what it feels like.'

He nodded, mercifully getting up from the sofa now and walking back over to the piano. She'd been having real trouble keeping her composure with him sitting so close and talking about something so intimate. It was a relief to have the physical space between them again.

Sitting down, he began to play what sounded like a piece of classical music, his long fingers skating elegantly over the keys.

'There are certain pieces of music and songs that are supposed to provoke more of a response than others. It happens when the music does something unexpected,' he said, segueing into a tune she realised she knew well.

'Is this "Hallelujah"?' she asked excitedly, sitting up straighter. She'd always loved this Leonard Cohen song.

He answered by beginning to sing the song in his beautifully gravelly voice, which of course suited it perfectly. She watched in fascination, noting how his body language was much more relaxed now that he wasn't performing for a bigger audience. His fringe fell down over his forehead as he dipped his head in concentration and she had the strangest urge to go over there and push it back from his face so she could see his eyes again.

As the emotion of the lyrics flooded through her she felt it again, that incredible rush of euphoria that started in her spine and cascaded out through her body in waves, making the entire surface of her skin stand up in goosebumps. It continued to wash over her, wave after wave of it, as he sang the entire song. The emotion caused tears to press against the backs of her eyes and throat and her insides to twist and swoop with poignant elation.

'Whoa!' she said, wiping away a tear that she hadn't been able to hold back at the close of the song. 'That was amazing.'

'Pretty cool, huh?' Alex said. The expression on his face made her suspect he'd been moved by it as well. She wondered fleetingly whether he'd been thinking about Tia and what he'd lost with her, before forcing the thought out of her head. It made her want to cry even more.

They sat there looking at each other for longer than was entirely comfortable, the intensity of the silence making her head throb and her chest ache.

'Well, I guess we ought to get to bed ourselves,' she said nervously, standing up and stretching. It seemed such a shame to leave the lovely warm living room now, especially when he was doing such a wonderful job of entertaining her with his playing, but it felt like the right time to turn in. In fact, she had a strong inclination to have a bit of time on her own now—to process the strange feeling of *yearning* for something elusive that was making her heart race and her skin prickle.

'I guess so,' Alex said, standing up too.

They walked to the bottom of the staircase together in silence.

'Straight to bed?' Alex asked, and she tried not to imagine that there was more to that question than he really meant.

'I think so, I'm pretty tired now,' she said, beginning to mount the stairs.

He followed her up, his presence like a benevolent shadow behind her.

When they reached his room and she turned back to say goodnight, she found he was looking at her with a strange speculative expression on his face.

'Well, goodnight,' she murmured, wondering what was going through his mind and knowing she'd be at a total loss if anyone asked her to explain how she was feeling right now.

'Thank you for inviting me here with you. I get how hard it must have been to bring me when things with Violet are so tense. I appreciate you telling me about it and trusting me with something so personal and challenging for you.' He took a small step closer. 'I had a really good time today,' he said, his voice a low rumble that made happy chills skitter along her nerves.

'You sound surprised,' she joked nervously, but he didn't smile back, just frowned a little.

Her throat felt oddly tense so she lifted her hand to massage it. He dropped his gaze to watch the movements she made.

'Well, goodnight. Have a good sleep. Don't let the bedbugs bite. And Merry Christmas,' she gabbled, dropping her hand awkwardly back to her side again.

He was looking at her with that strangely intense expression in his eyes again now. It was something she couldn't quite pin down. Something that made her insides swoop and soar.

Without saying a word, he pointed up at the mistletoe that was now hanging from the top of his room's doorway.

'I'm sure that wasn't there earlier,' he said, his lips quirking into a wry smile.

'Hmm, no. My mother is incorrigible.'

'Maybe it would be wrong to ignore it though.' He raised a teasing eyebrow. 'Isn't it bad luck or something?'

'I think you're getting it mixed up with not walking under ladders,' she said shakily.

'Ah, perhaps I am.'

'And I thought you only kissed very special people.'

His eyes widened. 'You heard all that between me and your sister, huh?'

'Yeah, I didn't mean to eavesdrop. I was…uh… just sitting near the door.'

He smiled, evidently not believing a word of it. 'I get the feeling it was something you needed to hear.'

'I guess it was.'

There was another small pause, during which the house suddenly seemed very quiet. So quiet she could hear the rapid thump of her pulse in her ears.

'Okay, well, just in case it is bad luck to ignore it—' she pointed at the mistletoe, then waggled her finger at his face '—I'm just going to kiss you on the cheek this time.'

But as she leaned forwards, angling her head so that her lips were aiming for the side of his face, he turned towards her and their mouths connected.

She drew back with a startled gasp. 'Oh! Sorry, I didn't mean to—' But he cut her off by sliding his hand into her hair and pulling her back towards him, pressing his mouth hard against hers again so deliberately that there was no way she could misconstrue it as an accident this time.

Her insides seemed to melt as he deepened the kiss, opening his mouth to slide his tongue against hers. It was a covetous kiss, full of need and determination. She sank into it, breathing him in, basking in the passion of his hunger.

When he finally released his grip on the back of her head and they drew apart, their mouths remained only centimetres from each other's. They stood there transfixed in each other's gazes, their breathing loud and guttural in the quiet corridor.

'What—? What's going on here?' she gasped, staring into his eyes in total astonishment.

'I'm kissing *you* this time,' he murmured, gazing at her with such fierce intensity her whole body flooded with desire. 'Is that okay?'

She blinked at him. 'Um… Er… Uh—yes. Of course. Yes, it's okay.'

Because it was. It really, really was.

The corner of his mouth lifted in a smile at her

inarticulateness. 'In that case, I'm going to do it again.'

She just nodded, not trusting herself to form any decipherable words this time. She let out a small gasp of pleasure as his mouth connected with hers again, his tongue sliding forcefully between her lips.

If she'd had any doubts about Alex being a good kisser they were totally quashed now. She'd never been kissed so intently, or so thoroughly. It made her toes curl with delight. His lips were soft but his mouth was firm against hers, his tongue gently exploring her mouth with possessive intent.

He pushed her gently backwards until she was pressed against the door to his room, his body hot and firm against hers, and she sucked in a breath as she felt just how into this he was.

'Perhaps we should take this inside,' he murmured against her mouth.

'Yes, yes, good idea,' she muttered back, fumbling for the door handle.

Once they were inside he lost no time in undressing her, slowly at first, then picking up speed as more and more of her body was revealed. She knew he'd seen most of it before when they'd gone swimming and she'd worn that skimpy bathing costume, but it didn't seem to stop him from wanting to reverently check out every inch of her now.

After finally shucking off his own clothes and standing still, quivering with barely controlled desire as she explored the smooth skin and the swell of the muscles on his chest and arms with her fingertips, he finally steered her back towards the bed. Urging her to lie back, he climbed over her and leaned down to kiss her mouth again.

He was so gentle with her, and so covetous, it took her breath away. She'd never felt worshipped like this before. Never felt so attractive. He kissed and touched every inch of her—some places much more thoroughly than others—and she sank back into the pure pleasure of it. Every part of her body felt connected. When he kissed her ankles she felt it in her belly, and when he moved up to press his mouth along her jaw, biting down gently on the sensitive skin there, it sent spirals of delicious sensation all the way down to her toes.

Then things got a little more intense. Then a little more, until the night blended into one big blur of pleasure and she lost herself in the kind of sexual fulfilment she'd never even dared to dream could exist.

CHAPTER NINE

So THAT WAS a fun night.

Alex lay in bed the following morning with Flora sleeping peacefully next to him, thinking that *that* had to be the understatement of the year.

The whole day had been incredible. From the deep connection he'd felt with Flora after gaining such a thorough insight into what drove her, to seeing the look of ecstasy on her face when he'd played music just for her last night.

Standing in front of his room, all he'd been able to think about was kissing her—not that the idea hadn't flitted through his head on a regular basis throughout the day. It had seemed inevitable that it would happen at some point, he mused. Clearly they were very attracted to each other and he was pretty sure Flora must have felt it too, considering the way she'd responded to him with such eagerness.

Last night he'd not allowed himself to think about how it would change things between them, unable to resist the overpowering desire to be close to her that had plagued him all evening—hell, all day. But, as he thought about it now, a niggle of alarm wound its way through him. Would she expect this connection to mean more than he was capable of right now?

He became aware of her stirring next to him and turned onto his side to smile at her as she started to blink open her eyes.

'Alex?' she murmured. He answered her with a gentle kiss, feeling her sleep-warmed skin heat his face.

'Good morning,' he said eventually, pulling back from her to see the smile he'd hoped for in her eyes.

She hid a yawn behind her hand, then grinned at him. 'A very good morning indeed.'

'Did you sleep well?' he asked, brushing a fallen eyelash from her cheek.

'I did,' she murmured. 'Did you?'

'Actually, I did for once. You wore me out,' he teased, grinning at her mock-reproving look.

'I think you'll find you were just as enthused as I was,' she said. He was relieved to hear her voice was only playfully stern.

'You're quite right, I was,' he said, bending forward to kiss her again.

When he drew back, she fixed him with a puzzled frown.

'What is this?' she asked, waving her finger between the two of them.

He stilled, genuinely not knowing how to answer that. His heart thumped hard in his chest. 'What do you think it is?'

'I don't know.'

'Do we need to put a label on it?' He held his breath, waiting for her answer.

'No,' she said slowly. 'Probably not.'

'It's unexpected, that's what it is,' he said, smiling in relief at her.

'Agreed,' she said, returning his smile. 'But if we did want to explain it—not that we need to—I guess it's just two friends comforting each other for the night at a difficult time in their lives?'

He nodded slowly, pushing away the unexpected sinking feeling in his gut. 'Yeah, sure,' he said, flopping back onto the pillows. 'Just a bit of friendly sex between…er…friends.'

He felt her shift beside him and she leaned over to push away a strand of his fringe that had fallen over his eyes.

He grimaced. 'I know, I should cut it,' he said, before she could.

'No. Don't,' she said, shaking her head. 'It suits you like that.'

'Still, it's about time I started taking a bit more care of my appearance again.'

'A shave might be good,' she said with a wry smile, delicately fingering her sore chin.

He rocked to one side, then rolled on top of her, taking her by surprise and making her gasp. 'Actually, I think the pink-chinned look suits you,' he said, bending forward to nuzzle her jaw, then kiss her throat, before moving back up to press his mouth to hers. 'It's very sexy,' he murmured against her lips.

'Hmm,' she purred as he shifted above her, making his intentions for the way he wished to spend the rest of the morning perfectly clear.

One night and one morning.

'I suppose I can put up with it for such a good cause.'

'Excellent. I love a martyr with no morals,' he teased, moving down to kiss her neck again. Then he moved lower, hearing her half giggle, half moan with pleasure in response.

How he loved that sound.

Afterwards they talked and laughed and talked some more about their lives and their pasts and about Amy, but not about what they were doing here together.

It was better that way. As he'd told her when she'd tried to set him up with her friend Lucy, he wasn't looking for anything serious at the moment and she was back off to the States soon anyway.

So friendly, consoling, unemotional sex was all it could be.

* * *

They eventually peeled themselves out of bed an hour later and Flora slipped back to her own room, thankfully not encountering anyone else on the way, and took a long, soothing shower. As soon as she was ready, she tapped on Alex's door and they went downstairs together to grab some much-needed breakfast, agreeing they'd go back to Bath after eating and saying goodbye to everyone.

Evan and Violet were in the breakfast room, gazing into each other's eyes with their fingers entwined. When Flora walked in her stomach did a strange lurch. Not because the sight of her sister and Evan still made her intensely jealous, but because she realised she didn't feel like that about the two of them any more. Being around Alex had made her aware that she no longer had romantic feelings for Evan. Her body didn't respond in any of the predictable ways it used to when he turned to look at her with his mesmerising golden eyes.

'Hi, Flora,' he said in his low, gravelly voice and she didn't even blink.

'Good morning. I'm surprised to see the two of you up this early. You're not exactly known for being early risers,' she joked good-humouredly, taking a seat opposite Violet.

'No, well, we had an early night,' Violet said with a glint of mischievous innuendo in her eyes.

'So you're back together?' Flora asked, deciding there was no point tiptoeing around it.

They both nodded, then turned to gaze into each other's eyes again. Flora suddenly understood how in love they were with each other. She'd seen signs of it at the wedding that she'd been forced to attend, but through her haze of drunkenness she'd not seen the utter transfixed devotion she saw now.

'I'm glad,' she said, and found she really meant it.

'Thanks, Floor, me too,' Violet purred, not taking her eyes off her husband for a second.

Penny came in then and Flora and Alex gratefully placed their breakfast orders with the housekeeper. As soon as Penny had gone, Flora's parents came in and they all got caught up in a discussion about music that lasted for the rest of the meal.

Flora found, with a swell of happiness, that she was having a really good time chatting with her family. It helped that Alex was by her side, covertly running his fingertips over the back of her hand under the table. Being this comfortable in the home she'd grown up in was something she had not experienced for a very long time.

'Anyway, we're going to hit the road,' she announced as soon as their plates were cleared. 'We've got a long drive ahead of us, especially with the roads so snowy.' Snow had settled over the whole country overnight and there were warnings about some roads being hazardous to drive on, which would make their drive back a lot slower.

There followed a flurry of activity where she and Alex packed up their bags and met everyone down in the hallway for a send-off. Her parents hugged them both and Alex complimented them on their fantastic hospitality and thanked them for including him.

'I'll take the bags out to the car and see you there,' he said to her, flashing her an encouraging smile.

Flora turned to her sister and held out her arms for a hug.

'I'm so glad to see things are progressing with sexy Alex,' Violet murmured huskily into her ear. 'It's amazing what a bit of rivalry and a sprig of mistletoe can incite.'

Flora drew back to raise an eyebrow at her. 'Was it you who hung it above his door?'

Violet shrugged casually, then smiled. 'I thought the two of you could do with a bit of encouragement.'

'Yes, well, we're still just friends, Vi. Neither of us are in any kind of emotional state for a relationship right now. And anyway, I'm back off to New York soon.'

'Uh-huh,' Violet said, looking and sounding completely unconvinced. 'Look,' she said, her expression becoming serious now, 'I know I've been a selfish cow in the past, Floor, but I genuinely want you to be happy.'

Flora became aware of her eyes filling with tears and blinked them back quickly. 'Thanks, Vi. I want you and Evan to be happy too. You're good together.'

Her sister appeared to be blinking back her own tears now. They had one more tight hug before Flora extricated herself and gave both her mother and father one last kiss on their cheeks.

'Thanks so much for having us. Merry Christmas.'

'Come back and see us again soon, darling,' her mother said, hugging her hard. 'We really miss you, you know.'

Flora nodded and said, 'I know. I miss you too. I'll be back soon.' Then she quickly walked out of the door before she began crying in earnest.

Alex was leaning against the car, waiting for her.

'Ready to go?' he asked with concern in his voice as he clocked her strained expression.

'Yes, I am,' she said, getting into the passenger side and clicking on her seat belt.

'Are you okay?' he asked as he got in beside her, turning to fix her with his bright, intense gaze.

Her stomach swooped as she gazed back at his handsome face, her eyes dropping to those firm lips she'd been kissing less than an hour ago. 'Actually, yes, more okay than I've been for a long time. I think Amy would have been pleased to see me getting on with my family so well. Pleased and relieved,' she added, flashing him a wobbly smile.

Alex grinned back with genuine warmth and pleasure in his eyes, then turned the key in the ignition, put the car into gear and set off back to Bath.

CHAPTER TEN

THE NEXT NIGHT Flora was kicking off her heels, desperate to give her poor aching feet a break after an intense day back at work, when her phone rang. Picking it up, she saw Alex's name on the screen and accepted the call with a swell of nerve-tinged pleasure. They'd texted a couple of times during the day about random things— clearly he'd been bored at home on his own, Flora had mused as she'd juggled emails and calls and demands from her staff and clients—but they hadn't actually spoken since he'd dropped her at home late on Boxing Day night.

'Hey, how was your day?' he asked without preamble. She really appreciated that. She had little enough energy as it was for conversation without being drawn into an awkward egotistical dance to see who could be the most aloof after a break from each other's company.

'A bit of a pig, if I'm honest,' she said, letting out a long sigh as all the tensions of the day came flooding back to her. Despite her hope that a break over Christmas would help her boss thaw to her a little, he still seemed determined to keep her right under his thumb.

'Still giving you trouble, is he?' Alex asked and she felt a rush of relief that he understood without her having to spell it out—and that it felt okay to complain to him about it. He'd been so lovely when she'd told him about how much she'd been struggling to keep her composure at work when they'd travelled back down to Bath the night before. He'd been both attentive and kind. Much like his sister had always been whenever she'd needed a pep talk.

'Yeah,' she said glumly. 'He's still treating me like I'm an idiot.'

'Okay,' he said, 'I'm coming over.' And he ended the call.

She stared at her phone for a good few seconds,

wondering whether she was so tired she'd just imagined that happening.

Her fears were allayed, however, when there was a ring on her doorbell a few minutes later. She opened the door to find Alex standing on the doorstep holding a chocolate cake in one hand and a bottle of wine in the other.

'Now there's a sight for sore eyes,' she said, ushering him inside and taking the bottle and cake from him so he could shrug his coat off.

'It sounded like you could do with some company, but if you'd rather I just handed over the refined sugar and alcohol and left you to indulge in peace I'll understand,' he said, following her into the kitchen.

'No way,' she said, putting the offerings onto the work surface. 'You're most welcome too.'

And he was. It was lovely to have someone to talk to about what had gone wrong with her day. Before Amy died it would have been her that she'd call—though only if it had been a particularly taxing day. Most of the time she just kept all the stress to herself, locked away deep inside her.

As she turned to face Alex he flashed her one of his alluring smiles and her insides swooped with pleasure. 'Well, good, because I could do with a friend tonight too,' he said.

'Really?' she asked, worried that he'd had a bad day as well and in her self-centred state she'd totally neglected to ask him about it.

'Yeah,' he said, moving slowly but very deliberately towards her. 'I missed your *friendly* company.'

Ah, now she got it.

She grinned at him, feeling a little shiver of excitement race down her spine as she took in the look of desirous intent in his eyes.

'And, as your friend, it's my duty to take your mind off work,' he said, starting to undo the buttons on her blouse.

She let out a long hiss of pleasure as he dipped his head to kiss her throat, then pushed the blouse off her shoulders.

'Hmm, how very altruistic of you,' she mumbled, drawing in a sharp breath as his nimble fingers made short work of unhooking the clasp of her bra, which he then removed in one swift movement.

Taking a step backwards, she realised he'd manoeuvred her against the kitchen island. She gasped as he slid his hands under her bottom and lifted her onto it, moving his body between her legs to lean in and kiss her hard.

He was less gentle with her this time, which was exactly what she needed. She soon forgot all about her horrible day, allowing herself to sink into the passion and intensity of his lovemaking.

Not that they were 'making love' per se, she reminded herself hazily.

No, they'd agreed that this was nothing like that.

For Alex, the next few days passed by in a blur of intensely pleasurable time spent with Flora in the evenings and intensely focused days of composing new songs, which seemed to flood into his head as soon as she'd closed his front door behind her on her way to work.

He'd thought a lot about what Flora had said

about how he was handling his music career and had come to the decision that he was going to make things happen for himself this next year, even if it killed him to do it. She was absolutely right—he couldn't just stay within the safe confines of the band in the hopes they'd have a breakthrough soon. He wasn't going to give up on his dream of going solo, no matter how hard that might be.

He wanted to play his own music.

Luckily, the band had agreed to take the week between Christmas and New Year off as a break in order to recharge their creative batteries so he was able to dedicate that time to working on his own material.

Near the end of the week he was confident enough in what he'd written to record it for a demo, so he called a friend in London who part-owned a recording studio and arranged to use a spare studio on the Friday. He didn't say anything to Flora about the new songs, wanting to surprise her with them at some point in the future.

For now, he just wanted to keep the momentum of his creativity going.

To his utter surprise and great delight, his friend knocked on the studio door at the end of his session and introduced him to a music producer who was working in the room next to him. After an involved discussion about the state of the music industry, the guy asked to sit in and listen to what he'd managed to record.

After hearing the songs Alex played him, the producer was hugely complimentary about the material. He asked to take a copy of the demo away with him to pass on to a colleague, who was apparently looking for an artist like him to complement his growing client list.

In Alex's adrenaline-fuelled creative haze it seemed entirely meant to be. Not that he was going to get too excited about it. He'd had enough knock-backs by now to know not to hope for too much to come out of it. Still, he was pleased with what he'd achieved that week and had a solid demo to send to other labels off the back of it.

Maybe this year *would* be his year.

Not wanting to go home to Bath on his own after finishing in the studio, he looked up the address for Bounce soft drinks and went to meet Flora after work.

He spotted her coming out of the building alone, her shoulders a little slumped and her brow pinched into a tired-looking frown.

That idiot boss of hers had a lot to answer for.

The flash of pure anger at how she was being treated propelled him forwards in a surge of protective indignation. He marched up to her, scooped her into his arms and planted a hard kiss on her mouth, wanting her to know that not everyone was oblivious to her charms.

'Alex!' she said, once he'd pulled back from the thoroughly intensive kiss he'd given her. 'What are you doing here?'

He loved that she looked so ridiculously pleased to see him and his chest gave a peculiar throb of pleasure.

'I've come to escort you home,' he said, linking his arm though hers. 'I thought we could go straight back to your place tonight to celebrate you finishing work for the year,' he said, grinning at her.

She nodded in a pseudo-sombre manner. 'I guess if we're going out to celebrate the New Year tomorrow with friends, a quiet night in might be just the ticket,' she said, snuggling closer to him.

'Who said anything about quiet?' he teased, his whole body flooding with desire at her responding look of unconcealed enthusiasm.

CHAPTER ELEVEN

SATURDAY NIGHT WAS New Year's Eve and, on Alex's insistence, Flora turned up to his place for a meal before they hit the pubs in town with Pete and Des from the band, who were going to be out with their partners.

She walked into his kitchen to find him cooking up a storm.

'Did you have a relaxing morning?' he asked as he turned away from the stove to drag her to him for a welcoming kiss.

She'd been at a spa all day, pampering herself with massages and beauty treatments galore—a suggestion of Alex's after she'd complained last night about how much her whole body was aching from sitting at her desk and on the train.

'Yeah, your magic antidote suggestion seems to have cured me. I no longer feel one hundred and ten years old.' She leaned against the work surface and watched him stir some seasoning into the food, wishing his talented hands were on her instead of the spoon and pan. 'I'm really not looking forward to going back to work after New Year,' she said, sighing. 'But at least I'm only there for another couple of weeks.'

'Is that when the project's due to end?' he asked, turning away from her to throw a couple of empty tins into the recycling box. Was it her imagination or was his body language a little tense?

'Yeah. Then I'm back off to my position in New York,' she said stiffly, moving closer so she could peer into the pan, feeling an uncomfortable urge to change the subject. She really didn't want to think about leaving right now. 'Hmm, is that chicken stew?'

'Coq au vin,' he said with a nod.

'Well, it smells delicious.'

'It's going to taste delicious too,' he said, with a cocky confidence that made her smile. 'I happen to be an excellent cook.'

'You're full of surprises,' she said, leaning back against the kitchen work surface again to give him an assessing glance.

There was a beat of silence.

'Is the stress really worth it?' he asked gruffly, making her wonder where the sudden vehemence had come from.

'At work?' she asked, her mind taking a moment to catch up with the meaning behind his question.

He nodded.

'I used to think so but, I have to admit, some days I wonder. It's pretty exhausting keeping up with the pace of it and I'm sick of having to work in the evening and weekends to catch up with myself.'

'Then give it up,' he said, waving the spoon at her. 'Make a change. Work for yourself. Break the routine and just do something different—something you feel passionate about.'

She stiffened, discomfort making heat rise to her face. 'But I've worked so hard to get where I am. I can't just give it up now.'

He studied her with an irritated frown. 'Of course you could. You just have to adjust your priorities.'

His insinuation that it would be easy to just give up what she'd spent years working for sent a prickle of exasperation up her spine. It wasn't as simple as that. It really wasn't. She was too used to the security she enjoyed working for Bounce now. It could take years to get to that same position if she set up her own business. And what if she failed? All her hard work would be wasted.

They glared at each other crossly, the air crackling with barely contained antagonism.

'I'm just going to use your bathroom,' she muttered, looking away from his maddening expression. The last thing she wanted right now was to have a row with him. She was here for some light relief, not a life lesson.

She was just about to come out of the bathroom, after taking a few deep, steadying breaths to calm her racing heart, when she heard voices in the hall. She froze on the spot, a sixth sense telling her not to go any further.

'Look, it's not a good time,' she heard Alex say.

'Okay, you win,' came the urgent tones of a woman's reply.

It only took Flora's brain a second to recognise those gravelly tones.

Tia.

'What are you talking about?' Alex asked, sounding exasperated.

A little voice in Flora's head cheered him on.

'It worked, Alex. You wanted to make me jealous and I am.'

'Tia, what—'

'Don't pretend you don't know what I'm talking about,' she cut in. 'Give me some credit at least.'

'Are you talking about Flora?' The incredulity in his tone sent a cold shiver rushing down her spine. So that confirmed the fear she'd been pushing to the back of her mind ever since that morning in bed in her parents' house. He hadn't been feigning nonchalance about what she meant to him; he really did only see her as a friend.

'Look, I know you were upset when I got together with Zane, but I was having a really hard time. He was there for me when you weren't!' Tia whined.

'My sister was dying,' Alex stated in a cold voice.

'And you just pushed me away when I tried to support you. You wouldn't even let me come and meet her. It was like I didn't even exist any more.'

'So you gave up on me and moved straight on to the next band member in line.' There was a break in Alex's voice that made Flora's breath catch.

'I'm not proud of how I handled it.' There was a long pause. 'I want you to know I'm sorry.' Another pause. 'And that I regret it.'

Flora's heart was beating so fast now she felt dizzy as she waited for Alex's response.

'You regret it?' Alex asked in a voice that seemed to have lost all its anger now.

'Yes. I want you back.'

There was a long pause. Flora was aware of her pulse thumping painfully in her throat.

'What about Zane?' he asked eventually.

A wave of nausea rose through her at the discovery that he could be so easily persuaded to give in to Tia's will, even after the callous way she'd acted towards him.

'He'll get over it,' Tia said in that cooing voice Flora had heard her use the first time they'd met and she'd thought she'd have to break up a fight between her two lovers.

'I… I don't know what to say,' Alex said gruffly.

There was a pause, then a strange *oof* sound, followed by a low moan of pleasure.

Flora felt her breath whoosh out of her. She took a couple of stumbling steps backwards, aware of her shoulder banging hard against the bathroom cupboard but not feeling the pain of it.

They were kissing, she was sure of it.

With heavy dread sinking through her, she crept forwards again to peek around the doorway into the hall. Alex and Tia were standing there with their arms twined around each other and their mouths locked together in a deep kiss.

Flora felt strangely spaced out, as if she was watching what was happening from afar, her emotions disconnected from what she was seeing.

Well, that's it then, she thought in a weirdly detached way. Alex was kissing Tia, which must mean he wanted her back.

But what about me? What about us?

She shook her head jerkily, pushing the dissenting voice out of her head. She was his *friend*. They'd agreed that whatever this thing was between them, it wasn't going to be serious.

Her hands had begun to shake. She crossed her arms and stuffed her hands under her armpits to calm the tremble in them.

It was Alex's life and his decision. She just wanted him to be happy. If that meant him getting back with Tia, then that had to be a good thing.

Didn't it?

Yes. *Yes.* He was in love with Tia and he'd been miserable without her.

Anyway, she was going back to America soon and she didn't want to leave him here on his own. She'd worked so hard for her powerful position and she couldn't give it all up now. She may not be beautiful and arty and alluring like Tia and

Violet, but she could hold her own in a tough business environment and she could damn well look after herself.

She didn't need a man to make her happy. She didn't need Alex.

Eyes burning and throat tense with a sudden swell of panic at being discovered eavesdropping on their reunion, she dashed back into the bathroom. Taking a few steadying breaths, she closed the door quietly behind her.

Her thoughts were racing so fast around her head that she felt dizzy and sick with it. She longed to get out of there and leave them to it. She knew they must have a lot to talk about and didn't want to cause any more trouble between them. Her heart lurched and her stomach churned at the thought of making an uncomfortable exit past them. She didn't think she could face Alex right now. She had no idea what she'd say to him. Her mind was whirling with thoughts and emotions and she didn't want to put him in an awkward position.

Yes, that was it. That was why she was feeling

so panicky and weird. The whole situation was highly emotionally complicated. Better to leave quietly and explain her absence later when they'd all had a chance to get their heads together.

Glancing round the bathroom, she feverishly eyed the small window above the toilet and decided it was probably just about big enough for her to climb out of. Putting down the lid of the loo, she put one foot on it and boosted herself up. Pushing the window open as far as it would go, she slid quickly out into the sharp wintry air, trying not to fall over the recycling bins stacked up directly beneath the window. She felt her trousers snag on something, then rip as she jumped down, but she didn't stop to check the damage. She'd do a full assessment once she was far enough away from this place, safely back at home.

After letting herself out through the back gate with a shaking hand, she traversed the lane out to the street and hightailed it back to her flat.

Well, you did it, she told herself as she unsteadily poured herself a large glass of white wine in her kitchen ten minutes later. Her whole body felt weirdly numb now. She'd fulfilled Amy's wish to make sure Alex was okay. He was a lot happier now than when she'd first met him. If a reconciliation with Tia was on the cards, his life would be firmly back on track.

She could go back to the States with a clear conscience.

Taking a big gulp of wine, she forced it past the tight pressure in her throat.

Yes, it was all looking very good for Alex.

So why did she feel like crying?

For maybe five seconds after Tia launched herself at him and pressed her mouth hard against his, Alex had allowed himself to sink into the familiar comfort of the kiss. Her taste and smell and touch brought back intense memories of happier times, making his chest ache and his taste buds tingle with nostalgia. But then a vision of Flora's smile had swum through his mind and kissing Tia had suddenly felt completely and utterly wrong.

Before Christmas he'd longed for things to go

back to the way they once were: before Amy had become ill, before his love of playing and writing music had deserted him, before Tia had left him. He missed that more simple time, when he was full of naïve excitement about all the possibilities that lay ahead of him.

But his life was different now. He was different.

He felt as if he'd grown up in the last few weeks.

While it was a powerful ego rush to experience the glory of winning Tia back, he realised in those jarring seconds that he didn't want her any more.

He wanted Flora—intensely and with a passion that he'd never experienced before. He felt that she understood him and that she genuinely cared about him. It wasn't all about her when he was with her, like it had been with Tia. Flora treated him as an equal.

That was who he really wanted in his life.

Flora.

He just needed to convince her that he was worth taking a risk on and staying here in England for.

After untangling himself from Tia's desperate grip and sending her on her way as fast as he could—which had proved a little tricky when it became obvious that she was intent on changing his mind, even going as far as producing tears, which had no effect on him whatsoever—he'd slammed the door shut behind her and rushed back to tell Flora about his revelation, only to find the flat empty.

He checked every room twice, desperately hoping he'd somehow missed her. But after a few minutes of calling her name—and experiencing a sick, sinking feeling when he noticed that the bathroom window was wide open—he came to the disturbing conclusion that she wasn't there any more. That she'd escaped out of a *window*.

But had she gone right after they'd had that tense conversation about her giving up her job or right after Tia had turned up?

Picking up his phone with a shaking hand, he called her number.

'Hey, where did you go?' he asked gruffly when she finally answered.

'I thought I'd make a silent exit so you and Tia could work things out without being interrupted.' Her strangely upbeat tone of voice sent a panicky sort of shiver across his skin.

'It didn't sound like I was her favourite person at the moment,' she went on before he could say anything, 'and I didn't want to disrupt what looked like a reunion?' She inflected her voice at the end to make it a question, the intrigued tone making it sound as if she was fishing for salacious gossip. It sounded as if she had seen them kissing—but she wasn't angry with him about it.

What the hell was this? Why did she sound so happy at the prospect of him getting back together with Tia? Did what they'd been through together recently really mean so little to her? Was she totally set on going back to her job and life in the States and forgetting all about him?

'She wants me back, apparently,' he said, trying to keep the hurt at her unexpectedly blasé reaction out of his voice.

'Well, it's great to hear she's finally come to her senses,' Flora said, her voice jokey now as if she was totally oblivious to how much pain this conversation was causing him.

Humiliation sank to the pit of his stomach as it occurred to him that maybe hanging around with him as a friend really had just been about fulfilling Amy's last wish. That it hadn't meant anything more than that to her. That *he* didn't mean more than that to her.

'You think I should take her back?' he asked tersely, digging his nails into his palms to keep the desperation he felt at this painful revelation at bay.

There was a small pause before she said, 'Well, I guess everyone deserves a second chance. It sounded like she was genuinely sorry about the way she'd handled it all. And it would make your life so much easier if you were back on good terms with her, with regard to staying with the band.'

Was there a slight wobble in her voice now, or had he just imagined it?

'True,' he said, clenching his fists harder.

'I think you should do whatever makes you

happy, Alex,' she said so breezily that he knew for sure now that she'd never change her mind about jacking in her job and staying in England. With him. It was clear she was standing aside so he could get back with Tia without any hard feelings between them.

That she didn't care enough to fight for him. For them.

He was glad now that he'd only hinted about her doing that earlier, rather than coming right out and saying it. What a humiliating and utterly devastating knock-back that would have been. The last thing he needed in his emotionally fractured state after losing Amy was another woman rejecting him.

'We'll still be friends though, right?' she asked. This time he definitely detected a slightly strained note in her voice. Did she think he'd totally drop her if Tia was back on the scene? Was that really how he came across to her? The idea made him feel sick.

'Of course we'll still be friends, no matter what happens,' he managed to force out. His head was swimming now, his thoughts and feelings a tangled mess.

'Great.' She took a deliberate-sounding breath. 'Anyway, I'm going to go. I've got a banging headache—a migraine, I think—so I'm going to cry off tonight. Wish everyone happy New Year for me, won't you?'

'You're not coming out now?' he asked, hearing the incredulity in his voice.

There was a small, tense pause. 'No. Sorry, I'll only be a killjoy if I'm not feeling well. You'll have a good time with Tia and your friends though, won't you.' It was a statement, not a question. 'Happy New Year,' she said, and with that decisive end to the conversation she cut the line.

He sat there for a while afterwards, staring at the wall, feeling a fresh new kind of grief pouring through him. The pain of having become so close to Flora, only to lose her so abruptly, made his heart ache. It felt like a death, even though he knew she'd still be out there somewhere, getting on with her life without him.

But then he should be used to losing the people he loved by now. It seemed he was destined to be alone.

Getting up shakily, he walked into the kitchen and reached for a tumbler and the bottle of whisky he kept stashed at the back of the cupboard. But just as he went to screw off the top, something stopped him. He didn't want to sink back into oblivion again. He wanted to feel. To relive all the joyful thoughts and discoveries he'd experienced whilst he'd been around Flora. To prod those emotional bruises.

To his surprise, he found that he wanted to compose a new song.

Flora threw her mobile across the room, watching with a sick sort of satisfaction as it bounced along the floor and came to rest against the stone fireplace.

There was a large crack in the screen. *A bit like my heart*, she thought wryly, though there was no real humour in this observation.

She had no idea how she'd said all those words

to Alex without howling with misery-filled frustration throughout the whole conversation.

It seemed clear from the rasp in his voice that he felt bad about dropping her after all they'd shared in the last couple of weeks. But he was still in love with Tia. That was perfectly obvious. And she really couldn't blame him for how he felt. She'd seen the tension in him at the gig when Tia had been around and the way he'd looked at her. And she knew Tia could probably make him happier than she could; they had much more in common with each other. He only kissed very special people, after all.

Anyway, she was used to being second best by now. It seemed to be her default position with the men she fell for. She and Alex weren't right for each other; they were too different. They'd just been each other's emotional prop during a difficult time. The thing between them had only happened because they'd both been sad and in need of some human contact. They'd understood and soothed each other's pain, but that was all it had been about. If it hadn't been for Amy's death, they probably wouldn't have even connected.

Alex and Tia, on the other hand, had something she never would.

They made music together.

CHAPTER TWELVE

NEW YEAR'S DAY was horrendous.

Flora spent most of it lying in bed, staring up at the ceiling, not having the energy or impetus to get up and do anything with her day off.

She couldn't stop thinking about Alex and what he might be doing with Tia. Had he taken her out last night to meet up with Pete and Des in the pub? That would make sense. Tia was part of the band after all. They all belonged together.

Finally managing to drag herself out of bed at lunchtime, Flora got up and made herself a strong cup of coffee, wincing as the heat of it burned her mouth.

Trailing into the living room, she turned on the TV and stared blankly at the news, her eyes gritty and tired from a poor night's sleep. She hated being alone in bed again. Even though they had only spent a week waking up next to each other, she'd grown used to having Alex's solid form there next to her. She'd loved being able to roll over and wrap herself around him in the night, feeling the soft rise and fall of his breathing against her chest as he slept.

And he seemed to have slept much better with her in the bed too. He'd not woken up after a couple of hours like he had been doing before Christmas. Or so he'd told her.

Tamping down on a fresh swell of misery, she flicked the channel over to one that was playing music videos. She needed to hear something upbeat and positive right now to pull her out of this painful vortex of despair.

How could she be feeling this distraught after only being with him for such a short time? she wondered as a surge of hot tears pressed at the back of her eyes and throat. Was it because she'd been using Alex to fill the gaping hole in her heart that his sister had left when she'd died?

No. That hadn't been it. No one could ever replace Amy, not even her twin brother.

She'd fallen for him in his own right, this scruffy, roguish, compassionate, frustrating man.

Somehow he'd opened up her eyes and made her start to value things she'd never put any store in before. Like music. Like having a family and a home to go back to whenever she needed it. He'd made her stop and think about what she'd taken for granted for far too long—a notion that she'd been incredibly resistant to accepting in the past, even when Amy had repeatedly pointed it out.

At the thought of having lost both Amy and Alex, anxiety rose like a venomous snake ready to strike. She fought it back, determined not to give in to the constricting band of fear in her chest. She took a few deep breaths, blanking her mind.

But thoughts of Alex still managed to creep back in.

He'd had a way of making her feel calm whenever he was around. Whole. Enough.

Though she didn't feel *enough* right now. Not when she had Tia to compete with.

Inadequate. That was how she actually felt.

Corporate success meant nothing to Alex and that was all she had going for her.

Tia was beautiful and talented and mysterious and had wrapped herself around Alex's heart like a vine. There was no way a woman like that was going to let someone as amazing as Alex go. She'd be a complete idiot to do that.

So what did that make Flora?

Choking back her tears, she got up and went to take a long hot shower, hoping the stinging heat of the water would distract her from the cold chill that had invaded her body ever since she'd left Alex's flat last night.

She was gently towelling dry her strangely sensitive skin when her mobile started to ring. She picked it up, glancing at the display and feeling her heart leap into her throat as she saw the name on the screen.

Alex.

She almost let it go to voicemail, before telling herself not to be such a coward. They were still friends and she didn't want to cut all ties with him, even if it meant only hearing from him now and again. It would be terrifically hard, but she'd deal with it. She was well-practised in dealing with grief now.

'Hi,' she said, forcing her voice to sound up-beat and breezy. 'Happy New Year.'

There was a short pause before he spoke. 'Happy New Year, Flora.' His voice was rough, as if he'd been out all night and only just woken up.

'So how was last night? Did you all have a good time?' she asked in a strangled voice, wrapping her arm tightly across her stomach to quell the uncomfortable ache there.

'I didn't go,' he said tonelessly.

Ah, of course not. He and Tia must have stayed in. They'd had some making up to do after all.

She fought back the swell of nausea this thought caused.

'Well, I slept through the whole thing,' she chirped, feeling like the biggest faker in the world. 'My head's a lot better now though, thank goodness.'

There was another pause on his end of the phone. 'Great,' he said.

Another beat of silence.

'So what's up?' she asked, feeling desperate to get this conversation over and done with now, before the hard sobs that were making her throat constrict painfully managed to escape and give her away.

'I just wanted to call and let you know my news.'

'Oh?' She held her breath, steeling herself to hear something about him and Tia.

'The band have been offered a recording contract,' he said.

She sucked in a breath of surprise, feeling genuinely pleased for him. 'Oh, wow, that's fantastic! When did you hear?'

'Just now. Tia's just finished talking to the record producer. Apparently we'll be expected to start touring around England pretty quickly to get our name out there.'

'I'm really happy for you, Alex. Make sure you

send me photos from the road,' she said, biting her lip to stop herself from letting out a sob.

So that was it then. He'd be off soon, touring with his girlfriend. She hoped if Amy was looking down on them right now she'd be pleased with what she saw unfolding here.

Perhaps if she hung onto that hope this horrendous feeling of anguish would go away and she could go back to her old life feeling satisfied that everyone was happy and their lives were sorted.

Everyone except for her.

Because she was in love with Alex Trevelyan, and he didn't love her back.

After concluding the call, Alex put the phone down and swallowed hard. It had taken all his courage to tap on Flora's name to connect him to her, but he was glad he'd done it. He'd wanted to hear her voice again. He'd dreamt about it. He was missing her as if one of his major organs had been ripped out of his body, and it didn't take a genius to figure out which one.

She'd sounded so happy for him about the

band's contract that he'd not been able to bring himself to ask the questions that had plagued him all night, keeping him awake till the early hours.

Don't you care about me at all?

Would you be willing to stay in England for me?

Do you love me like I love you?

But of course he'd not asked her a single one of them.

He couldn't see any way to persuade her he was worth taking a risk on—that he could provide just as fulfilling a life for her here in England as her high-powered job did in the States.

She'd never intended to stay here long-term, so why would she change her mind now?

He remembered how she'd laughed about what an odd couple they'd make when he'd first met her. But did she really still feel like that after everything they'd shared?

He certainly didn't. It seemed completely clear to him now that they were actually perfect together. They complemented each other, made each other think and experience things in a totally new way. That had to be a good thing. Didn't it?

He certainly thought so. He knew now that he wanted Flora in his life, challenging him and making him feel things he'd never felt without her. But he was keenly aware that if he wanted her to stay—and he really did, so much it made his head throb—just like with his musical career, he was going to have to take some risks and work damn hard for what he really wanted.

And never, *never* give up.

CHAPTER THIRTEEN

A FEW DAYS LATER, Flora let herself into her flat after another long, gruelling day at work. To her huge relief, the UK launch was finally live and the whole frustrating project was over and done with so she could finally get her life back. As she walked inside she noticed a small padded envelope lying on the mat below her letter box. She guessed that her upstairs neighbour must have posted it through for her so it didn't get lost in the jumble of junk mail by the door in the communal entryway.

There was something about the shape and size of it that made her heart beat faster. Tearing off the top of the envelope, she turned it on its end and shook it, watching a recordable CD case slip out of it into her hand. There wasn't a note inside, but scrawled across the inner slip under the clear case were the words:

This one's for you, Flora.
Love, Alex

Hands trembling, she went over to the stereo system that had come with the flat and slid it into the CD drawer.

She'd expected to hear Nina Simone or Billy Holiday or even Leonard Cohen—as a reminder that they'd always be friends perhaps. So when Alex's beautiful gravelly voice started playing through the speakers the blood rushed so quickly to her head she had to sit down and take a few calming breaths. Her heart thumped hard in her chest as she listened to every single song on the disc, unable to move as the beautiful piano music washed over her and his voice moved through her like a pain-relieving drug.

And she had tingles *everywhere*.

As she concentrated on the lyrics, her earlier euphoria began to drain away as she realised she was listening to Alex singing love songs about a woman who had beguiled and inspired him. Someone who had made him feel music in his soul. Tia. The songs had to be about her.

And then the final song came on and it was explicitly clear that this one was about someone else entirely.

Amy.

The lyrics were so loving and poignant that tears rushed to her eyes. She sat there, paralysed with grief, sobbing hard as memories of her friend whirled through her head in a dizzying kaleidoscope of images.

Alex had put into words exactly how it had felt to lose her best friend.

It made one thing starkly clear. He completely understood her.

Just like Amy had done.

Getting up on wobbly legs, she went over to the drawer where she'd been keeping Amy's letter recently, carefully lifting it out, then smoothing it down on the dining table to read it. Her gaze skimmed over the beginning until she got to the part she was looking for:

I'm so proud of you for all that you've achieved. I always knew you'd be successful in whatever you did, but your drive and determination have astounded even me. I know you probably won't take a minute to step back and see the enormity of what you've accomplished, but get this: you truly are an incredible person, as well as the kindest, most generous woman I've ever had the pleasure of knowing.

She'd always skipped over that part before, racing to get on to the favour Amy had asked of her, but now she stopped to think about what her friend had been trying to tell her: that she could have whatever she wanted if only she put her mind to it.

If she wanted to branch out and start her own business, then she could do that. She certainly had the experience and knowledge to make her own initiative a success. She'd not done it up till now because she'd been afraid to leave the safe confines of someone else's business.

But it was time to stop being safe and move

on to the next stage of her life. One she was in total control of. If she found herself working with someone who didn't treat her with the respect she deserved, then she'd no longer work with them. Simple as that.

She was going to be her own woman from now on.

Excitement fizzed through her at the thought of it, lifting her beleaguered spirits. Yes, she was going to start acting like the woman Amy had always seen her as.

It was time to stop blaming her feelings of inadequacy on other people and take stock of her life.

If that meant starting her own business—just like Alex had suggested on New Year's Eve— then she'd do it on her terms and build it entirely from her own blood, sweat and tears.

Make it something to be truly proud of.

After meeting Alex and enjoying living in Bath, then making peace with what had happened with Violet and her family, she'd started having serious reservations about going back to her job in the States anyway. Perhaps this was the right time to move permanently back to England.

What was there in New York for her now anyway? A few friends she'd made over the last year or so, but no one particularly close. Not like Amy. Certainly no one like Alex. He was one of a kind.

She loved that about him.

Taking a breath, she pushed back her shoulders. Yup. She loved him.

And even if she couldn't have him, she wasn't going to let that stop her from taking the rest of her future into her own hands.

Alex was her friend and always would be, she hoped, and she wanted to let him know that she'd always be there for him too. She needed to tell him that, even if it would be the most painful, heart-wrenching thing she'd ever done.

She also wanted him to know how much he'd inspired her to make some positive changes in her life.

Yes, telling Alex all about her plans would be exactly the right thing to do to cement them.

But she didn't want to do it over the phone. She wanted to look him in the eye and say it.

Giving her face a quick scrub in the bathroom, she decided not to bother putting make-up on. He genuinely didn't seem to care whether she wore it or not. In fact, he seemed to prefer her looking natural and unconcealed.

Striding into the hall, she pulled on her boots and grabbed one of her coats from the peg, not even stopping to check whether it matched with the rest of her outfit, then let herself out of her flat.

She walked quickly towards Alex's place, hoping he'd be in and on his own. She didn't fancy saying her piece in front of Tia, but now she'd made up her mind she didn't want to lose the momentum of her decision either.

When she finally reached his door, she rang the bell for a good few seconds to make sure he heard it. Waiting impatiently, she tapped her foot and drummed her fingers against her legs, her heart thumping hard in her chest.

She was a little breathless from walking so

fast, and probably from the adrenaline rushing through her blood too. She took a couple of moments to compose herself, wanting to seem cool and relaxed when he opened the door.

After what felt like eons she heard the lock turn and the door swung open to reveal the breathtaking sight of Alex looking rumpled, but ridiculously sexy, in a T-shirt and jeans. His feet were bare, as if he'd just thrown on clothes after rolling out of bed.

'Sorry,' she said instinctively, 'I hope I didn't disturb anything.' Her insides did a slow, uncomfortable somersault as it occurred to her that he might have left Tia in bed.

He frowned at her, then rubbed at his eyes as if he thought he was imagining her there.

'Flora. You're here.' He said it as if he'd been waiting for her to come and was relieved that she'd finally arrived.

'Er… I just thought I'd pop over to say thanks,' she gabbled, a little panic-stricken by the thought of Tia overhearing them.

He stared at her with a bemused frown on his

face, then rubbed a hand over his eyes, looking thoroughly exhausted.

'Sorry, I was asleep on the sofa. Thanks? For what?'

He'd been asleep on the sofa? So he was alone then. Relief flooded through her. 'For the music you sent me,' she said, giving him a grin that she had to work hard for.

His perplexed expression cleared, to be replaced with a dazzling smile. 'And not just any music,' he said. 'Every one of those songs was written by me.'

Her heart did a slow flip. 'I thought I recognised your dulcet tones and I suspected it was your work. There was something about the songs that felt very *you.*'

He nodded thoughtfully. 'Want to come in?' he asked, sounding a little uncertain.

She hesitated, but only for a second. Now that she was here she really didn't want to leave until she'd told him about her epiphany.

'Er…yes, great,' she said, stepping into the hallway, aware of her legs trembling with nerves.

He led the way into his flat and took her coat from her, then gestured for her to go through to the living room.

'Want a drink?' he asked.

She suspected from his slightly antsy manner that he was hoping she'd refuse.

'No, thanks.' She sat down on his sofa and breathed in the wonderfully familiar smell of him as he sat down next to her.

'So what did you think?'

'About the songs?'

'Yeah.'

She could tell from the anticipation in his face he was desperately hoping she'd liked them.

'They're wonderful,' she said truthfully. 'Very moving. In fact they all gave me *frisson* and a couple of them made me cry.'

'Really?' He seemed ridiculously pleased to hear he'd been able to turn her into a blubbering, overemotional wreck.

'Yeah, proper ugly crying.'

'That's great,' he said, flashing her his gorgeous smile again, making her drag in a painful breath at the heart-wrenching sight of it. She'd missed seeing it *so much* over the last week.

'So I have some news,' he said, shuffling back on the sofa.

'Oh? About the band?' she asked, bracing herself for him to say it was actually about him and Tia.

'No, not the band. About the songs I gave you. I've started sending them out to record labels to try and get my solo career off the ground.'

'Really? That's fantastic news! Good for you!' Despite her heartache she still felt a rush of joy for him. 'Amy would be so proud of you,' she added.

His brow crinkled into a frown. 'Yeah, I'd like to think so.'

Flora took a breath, wanting to get the painful part out in the open and over and done with. 'So I guess you're going to be really busy, touring with the band soon too.'

'I've resigned from the band.'

She stared at him. 'Really? But what about

Tia? Won't it make it hard on your relationship if you're both off doing different things?'

His frown deepened and he crossed his arms over his broad chest. 'I'm not in a relationship with Tia. I told her I wasn't interested in getting back together.'

The room seemed to lurch from under her. 'When?' Her voice shook on the word.

'On New Year's Eve.'

'What? But it looked like—' She paused and swallowed, remembering the piercing pain she'd felt in her chest at the sight of the two of them kissing.

He uncrossed his arms and sat forwards, closer to her. 'I did consider taking her back, but only for a second and only because she was still going to be here when you were primed to jet back to the States.'

She blinked at him, her brain having trouble catching up with what he was saying. 'But you were kissing her,' was what came out when she was finally able to speak.

He shook his head. 'She kissed me. And yes—'

he held up his hands '—I kissed her back, but only because she took me by surprise. I realised straight away what a total idiot I'd be to even contemplate getting back with her when I could have you. There was never any contest.'

The room lurched again. 'Really?' She could barely breathe with excitement.

'Yes. Really.'

'But those songs you sent me—'

He raised his eyebrows. 'Yes?'

'I thought you'd written them about Tia.'

He gave her a look that said, *Don't be an idiot.*

'They're the songs I wrote right after Christmas, when things were so good between us. You inspired them. They're about *you*, Flora.'

'But…but…they're love songs.'

'Yes. Exactly.'

She was trembling all over now. 'So you're saying—'

'Yes. I love you.'

He moved towards her and slid his hand against her jaw, cupping her face so she had to look at him.

'I don't just want to be your friend, Flora. I want to have a proper relationship with you. I know it's all happened so fast, but I've never felt so sure of anything in my life.'

'Wow.' She swallowed hard, her head spinning. 'I want us to be more than friends too. I think I have since the moment I saw you stroll into the Pump Room.'

'Looking like a vagrant,' he teased.

Heat rose to her face. 'Yes, well, I'm not exactly proud of myself for the way I acted then.' She gave him a beseeching smile. 'But we all have our faults, right?'

He smiled. 'Absolutely. I know I do. I don't know what I was thinking, expecting you to just give up everything you'd worked so hard for to be with me.' He shook his head. 'I was being totally selfish. I'm the one that should be flexible because it doesn't matter to me where we live. I can write and rehearse and record music anywhere. Technology makes it easy to do that now. And I can easily jump on a plane to perform somewhere when I need to.'

'You'd really do that to be with me?'

'Like a shot.' He stroked his thumb against her cheek and she felt the affection in it right down to her toes. 'If you want I'll move to New York. Whatever it takes to be with you.'

Heart racing with excitement, she gave him a wide, tearful smile. 'Actually, I came over here to tell you I've decided I'm going to set up my own business. Probably here in Bath to begin with. So I'm going to hand in my notice at my job in New York.'

He matched her smile with one of his own. 'Well, that's perfect, because I'm going to need someone to take care of my brand. Someone who really understands me.'

She blinked at him. 'You mean me?'

He shrugged. 'Sure, why not? I can't think of anyone whose hands I'd be safer in. I know you'd do everything in your power to make sure every-thing is perfect.'

'So what you're saying is that my perfectionist tendencies might actually be quite useful?' she teased, with tears pooling in her eyes.

'Yes, in this case, they really will be.'

'Well, it's nice to hear you finally admit it,' she said, grinning like a fool.

'Hmm,' he growled, pulling her in for a kiss and not letting her go until she was breathless and dizzy from it.

'You really love me?' she asked, not wanting to believe it until he'd confirmed it for her.

'Yes. I love you,' he said forcefully. 'You've brought me back from the darkest place I've ever known and made me want to live again. Really live.'

'Me too,' she whispered, her throat clogged with tears. She really meant it too. She'd been at her lowest ebb when she'd first met him, but now she could see a bright and shiny future ahead.

With him.

The man who had showed her that life was really worth living and that she deserved to be put first.

The man she loved and who loved her back.

EPILOGUE

One year later

THEY SAT IN front of a roaring fire with the Christmas lights twinkling on the large Douglas fir in the corner of the room and opened the presents they'd bought for each other: her and Alex, her mother and father, and Violet and Evan, plus the good-sized bump in Violet's stomach.

Diana lifted up the framed photo of Flora and Alex that they'd given her, which showed the two of them with their arms slung around each other and broad smiles on their faces, standing in front of the new sign to Flora's marketing business in Bath, and gave a squeal of delight.

'I'm so proud of you, my clever girl,' she said with real happiness in her voice. 'This will be given pride of place on top of the piano,' she added, already getting up to place it there reverently.

'This is for the both of you,' Alex said, handing the present he'd brought for Flora's parents over to her father.

Francis opened it and lifted it up to show his wife with a look of pleasure on his face. 'Look, Diana, a signed copy of our daughter's famous boyfriend's chart-topping album,' he said with a grin.

'Ooh, how lovely!' she said, coming over to give Alex a tight hug. 'We're so proud of you too,' she murmured. 'We'll listen to that whilst we eat our supper, but perhaps you could play the piano now and we'll have a bit of a sing-song?'

'Sure, I'd love to play,' Alex said. 'I just need to do something upstairs first.' He turned to Flora and gave her one of his disarming smiles. 'I'm going to need you for this,' he said.

'Oh, yeah?' Violet drawled, giggling and waggling her eyebrows at them.

'Excuse us,' Flora said, getting up to follow

him out of the room, heat rising to her cheeks as she wondered what he had in mind.

Whatever he wanted would be fine by her though.

As they ascended the stairs she wondered again, as she had every now and again over the last year, whether her best friend had meant this to happen all along—for her and Alex to get together. Not that it mattered either way. She felt sure Amy would be pleased for them if she was able to look down from where she was and see how happy they were.

At the top of the stairs Alex stopped under the door frame of the guest room he'd stayed in the previous year, the room they'd first made love in. He pointed out the sprig of mistletoe that hung there once again.

'It looks like someone's been playing Cupid again,' he said with a grin.

'So it does,' she replied, walking into his arms and giving him a long and very satisfying kiss.

'Isn't it bad luck not to ask the person you love to marry you under the mistletoe?' he murmured against her lips. Before she could answer, or even draw in a startled breath, he dropped to one knee and pulled out a small velvet box from the pocket of his trousers and looked up at her.

'Flora, my muse, my lover, my friend—will you marry me?'

She stared at him, then at the beautiful diamond ring he showed her as he flipped open the box.

'Yes,' she whispered, her throat tight with exhilaration. 'Nothing would make me happier than being married to you.'

He stood up and took the ring out of the box, sliding it onto her finger with trembling hands.

'You bring the music, Flora Morgan, and I love you for it,' he said, leaning in to place the lightest of kisses onto her lips, sending her head spinning with pure joy. 'Now let's go celebrate by doing what everyone thinks we really came up here to do,' he said with a wink and a teasing smile. And as Flora giggled with happiness he guided her gently back into the room and shut the door firmly behind them.

* * * * *